Road to You

HARPER BLISS

lady lit_ publishing

Also by Harper Bliss

Far from the World We Know
Seasons of Love
Release the Stars
Once in a Lifetime
At the Water's Edge
French Kissing: Season Three
French Kissing: Season Two
French Kissing: Season One
High Rise (The Complete Collection)

For my wife, always.

PROLOGUE

1980

Children's cries echo between the walls around the kindergarten playground. It's a chaotic hive of activity. At the foot of the slide kids are being corralled into a somewhat orderly line by an attendant, so each gets his or her turn on the second-long ride down before crashing on the padded ground at the end. They scramble back up and join the back of the line for another go.

A few boys are kicking around a soccer ball, trying to keep it within their circle. But their five-year-old foot-to-eye coordination mostly fails them and one of them has to chase the ball down after every other kick.

In a corner of the playground, under an old oak tree, two girls sit next to each other. They are not interacting, just sitting side by side, each minding her own business.

One of them is looking up to the sky, singing a song of her own invention, as she twists one of her dark braids around her finger.

The other one, with short blonde hair, is collecting leaves and acorns, stacking them up neatly in equal piles. "Do you want to play?" she asks.

"What are you playing?" the braided girl counters.

"I'm the shop owner and you're the customer. You want to buy some acorns and the leaves are money."

"That's boring." She pauses and thinks. "I want to come into your shop and sing a song."

"No," the blonde girl replies. "This is not a song shop. You have to buy acorns and pay with money."

The braided girl looks at her with tilted head, and gets up. "I don't want to play then," she says and runs off, singing at the top of her voice.

The blonde girl looks after her for a few seconds, before getting back to her counting of leaves and acorns.

PART ONE

1996

CHAPTER ONE

KATHERINE

I look at Grace and I know it will end soon. She's just not right for me. I can't put it into words just yet. I'll need to suffer in silence for a while first. But I will tell her soon. Although, sitting here with her now, in her off-campus apartment on East Fourth Street, and seeing how the late afternoon sun catches in her hair, I foresee a difficult break-up.

She looks up from her book. "Pussycat," she says.

Reflexively, I roll my eyes at her. "What?" I hate it when she calls me that. It started with just Kat, though I told her from the very beginning that my name is Katherine, not Kat, and certainly not Pussycat.

"Got your claws out again?" She smiles a disarming smile.

"I told you before," is all I say.

"But you do everything a cat does." She doesn't let it go. "You purr when I pet you. You ignore me when I want you to look at me the most. And you've got very sharp claws. You even growl when you're unhappy." She rakes her fingers through her hair the way she does. She had it cut short this summer, before we returned to university, despite me begging her numerous times over the phone not to. When I saw her again after those long weeks during which she visited her family in Florida, I had to admit she had done the right thing.

"What did you want to ask me?" I ignore her comment, though I know she's right. My claws have become a little sharper every day for the past few weeks.

"I just wanted to say something." Grace's voice is always high, in a pleasant way. "I love you, Pussycat." She reaches out her hand and her fingers find my back, caress my skin.

"I love you too," I say automatically. It's not a lie. I love Grace. I never thought I would, but she wormed her way into my heart. But ten months together, and me as good as living with her instead of in my dorm room, have muted the passion I used to feel for her. Even though ours was definitely not a love-at-first-sight, thunderbolt kind of attraction. At least not for me.

Grace never questions my love. She's not a questioning kind of person. She just assumes things very easily. Like me not holding it against her when she arrived twenty minutes late for our first date—a date *she* instigated. I hid it well back then.

We're too young to stay together, anyway. I'm only a junior at NYU, she a senior. When it comes to romance, we're mere babies. Though I do consider her my first true love. The first one that matters.

"You're driving me crazy, Kat," Grace says. "You're looking at me all funny and you're making me wonder what you're thinking."

I quirk up my eyebrows. It's not like Grace to say things like this. Then again, it's not like me to have the thoughts I've been having. I try to remember when I started getting an inkling of our relationship nearing its end. Was it when she spilled coffee all over my French text book and I lost it? Or when I spotted her chatting animatedly to another girl in her Women's Studies class—a girl whom I know for a fact has had a crush on her all year—and I didn't experience any pangs of jealousy? Instead, I figured she'd find a rebound person easily when things between us didn't work out.

"I'm just nervous about this assignment. You know how much I regret taking French as an extra credit, but now I'm stuck with it and I'll be damned if I'll let it ruin my GPA."

"At least Seabolt's a looker," Grace says, again not questioning me further.

"You think?"

"Do you have eyes in your head?" Grace replies. "She's by far the hottest professor on campus. She makes me wish I had taken French."

"She has these thin lips and pinched-together mouth. And her eyes have this eery light color. I just find her frightening, that's all." I'm also not in the habit of thinking of my professors as hot.

"There's a rumor going around that she's one of us. Marcy claims she's seen her being very friendly with a certain female student." Grace sits up a bit. Topics like these always get her extremely excited.

"Marcy *would* say that."

"Why would you say that?" Her tone is snappy now. "I don't get why you don't like Marcy."

"She's just… too much for me. Too in-your-face. Too radical and militant."

"Do you know where we would be without other people being militant for us?"

Here we go again. Grace spends way too much time with her fellow students. This kind of stuff is all they talk about for hours on end. Then she gets upset because I don't like hanging out with her friends. Wanting to end this conversation as soon as possible, I hold up my hands in supplication. "Yes, Grace. I do know. I know all about it." Damn it, that sounded way more condescending than I had anticipated.

"Whatever," Grace says, and looks away.

I have to suppress the urge to up and leave. It's

Saturday and my roommate will be out. I could have a perfectly relaxed evening on my own—minus the laboring over the presentation I have to give in my French class on Monday. Choosing French was a frivolous choice for me, but I honestly believed it would round out my education well. I also didn't want to be an American who only ever wants to speak their mother tongue.

I love watching French movies, especially older ones with Catherine Deneuve, and my first girlfriend introduced me to the music of Jacques Brel. I just wanted to understand, without the help of a dictionary, what he was singing about. I'm not one to make a decision without thinking it through and examining the results from every angle. I found zero downsides to taking French. What I hadn't expected was that learning a new language seems to be a million times more difficult for me than for everyone else in my class. I stumble over every word. I can learn the vocabulary all I want, and revise the grammar all night long, but I'll never be a fluent French speaker. I've racked my brain trying to figure out why—as I tend to do—and the best explanation I can come up with is that I simply don't have a knack for languages. Which is why my major is Economics.

"What do you want to do tonight?" I ask, because I need to stop thinking about my French class, this assignment, and the prospect of Professor Seabolt's disappointed glare.

"TV and takeout?" Grace offers.

I nod my assent, though I can easily think of a dozen more exciting things to do with my Saturday night, but this is what we do now. We stay in and watch a TV movie. Eat too much and drift off into sleep without even considering the prospect of touching each other.

The thing about Grace is that I don't want to lose her. We know plenty of people who've remained friends after breaking up. With this as my objective, I'd better end it with her before she starts hating me.

ALI

"Ali, Ali, Ali." Anna shakes her head at me. "Will you never learn?"

"I'm in college so I learn plenty every day." I tuck a strand of hair behind my ear.

"You don't seem to pick up on what matters, though." Anna scrunches her lips together. "How old is she, anyway? How long have we known each other? You usually don't have affairs with women above twenty-five." She shakes her head again.

I probably shouldn't have told her. I wouldn't have—as I said to Julianne earlier, I can keep a secret—but Anna mentioned the rumor that's going around campus and then I guess she could just read it on my face. "I've decided to broaden my scope," I declare jokingly. "She's only forty-one."

"Jesus, Ali." Anna twirls a strand of ginger hair around her finger as she looks at me. Her coffee must have gone cold by now. "How did it even happen?"

I bite my lip and lock my gaze on her. "I've been told I have a certain… inviting kind of look in my eyes. She must have noticed."

"Nu-uh. I'm not falling for that. There's too much on the line for a professor who sleeps with a student for her to have just fallen for your pretty face like that. You must have pursued her. I know you well, remember?"

"Let's just say I needed some extra guidance on the subject of the French Revolution. For instance, did you know that Thomas Jefferson was the U.S. Minister to France during the revolution?" I know I'm driving Anna crazy with this. She's too strait-laced to get it. Most people are.

"Do you have an end game in mind?" Anna ignores my knowledge about this particular topic. "And what if the rumor spreads?"

I play with the gold bangle on my wrist. "My conscience is clear." I lean back in my chair and rest my ankle on my knee. I get a flashback from last night, when I sneaked into Julianne's house long after dark. I should be tired today, but I'm not.

"Do you have feelings for her?" Anna grimaces after taking a sip from her coffee.

Finally an interesting question. "I'm not indifferent to her, or what she thinks of me." A slow smile creeps along my lips. "It's just such a thrill, you know, to sit in class and watch her explain something while remembering the delicious noises she produced the night before. While nobody has a clue. And when her eyes land on me, which they always do at some point, to have this secret between us. It's intoxicating."

"For now," Anna says. "But you can't be so naive to think there won't be consequences. You could get expelled for this."

"No way." Though my tone of voice sounds certain, a flicker of doubt runs through me. "Both my parents are alumni. And we all know how generous the Wests can be."

"Your father would have a heart attack if he found out." Genuine worry crosses Anna's face. I do wish she would lighten up. It's just an affair.

"Then he would have my mother at hand to make him better." I drop my foot to the floor and plant my elbows on the table between us, staring deep into Anna's eyes—knowing it will unsettle her.

"Are you rebelling against the establishment because of your perfect upbringing?" Anna looks away. She's not really one for prolonged eye contact.

"Perfect?" I huff out an offended breath. "I dare you to try and be a West for a month. You'll soon notice exactly how perfect things are in my family."

"It must have been hard growing up in that huge house on the Upper East Side, having to walk all of two blocks to get to Central Park."

"Dear Anna." I grab her by the wrist. "You're my best friend in this whole wide wretched world, and I love you dearly, but why are you on my case so much today?"

"Because," Anna says, "I think you like her more than you let on and you might get hurt."

I sigh deeply. "When was the last time you saw me get hurt by a chick?"

"That's just the thing, though. She's not"—she curls her fingers into air quotes—"a 'chick'. She's your professor. She's in a position of power."

"As you said earlier," I retort, though I still fail to see why I'm getting the third degree about this, "she's the one who could lose her job over this. She's the one taking the risk. While I truly appreciate your concern, there's no need to worry about the future state of my heart. We're both consenting adults."

"I'm just worried, Ali. I can't see this ending well."

"We both know you worry too much." Anna spends most of her day worrying. About the cowlicks in her hair. About the A minus she got for an English Lit assignment. About what my parents thought of her when she came to dinner. About how her mother is coping upstate, even though Anna has been in college for almost two full years. "Are you coming to my gig tonight?"

"I don't know. I want to, you know that. But I have to write an essay by Tuesday and I only have fifteen hundred words so far."

"Fifteen hundred words? I've never written anything longer than a thousand words at the most. You try too hard, Anna." I tap my fingers against her arm. "Come to the gig tonight and I'll hook you up with Jennifer. She's been asking for you."

Anna turns up her nose at this. "If you want me to come out, you're gonna have to do better than try to tempt me with Jennifer."

"What's wrong with Jennifer?" I let go of her arm and lean back again.

"Apart from the fact that she's probably hit on half, if not more, of the female population at NYU, I know for a fact that the only reason she's even remotely interested in me is because I won't give her the time of the day. She's immature and crass."

"Why don't you tell me what you really think?" I give a chuckle. Jennifer accompanies me on acoustic guitar when I have a gig, and she's even more of a player than I am. I shrug. "It was worth the try. For what it's worth, she's a great friend."

"Please don't tell me she plays the guitar for you for altruistic reasons. Being on stage with you just gets her more pussy." Anna states this so matter-of-factly, I burst out laughing.

"Come for *me* then?" I bat my lashes at her. "We'll make a night of it. It's Saturday. You shouldn't be working on an essay."

"Are you playing anything new? Because I've heard all your songs a million times." Despite her petulance, I know Anna will be there tonight.

"We've been practicing a new cover. One of your favorite songs. But you have to come see which one it is for yourself." Anna never fell for my advances either. However, after she told me off in no uncertain terms, she did take a different shine to me. We've been friends ever since.

"Who am I to resist the pleading Alison West look? Those hooded eyes, that crooked smile, who can possibly be impervious to that?" Anna jokes. "Of course, I'll be there."

I shoot her one of my crooked smiles, secretly glad that we never ended up in bed together. Because if we had, I might not have Anna Davis as my best buddy. Tonight, I'll dedicate my cover of "Anna Begins" to her.

CHAPTER TWO

KATHERINE

I hate myself for still sitting here across from Grace. I keep telling myself—fooling myself—that a perfect opportunity will present itself for me to say that I've fallen out of love with her, but I now realize that there will never be a good time for me to look my girlfriend in the eyes and give her that information. Especially because she keeps going on about doing something special for our one-year anniversary less than a month from now. She wants to go to some cabin in the woods upstate for a weekend and the mere thought of it horrifies me so much, I almost told her tonight. Almost.

Even the lentil soup she's spooning into her mouth somehow manages to offend me. What is going on with me? Every single morning when I wake up, with her next to me or not, I decide that this can't go on. But as the day progresses my resolve crumbles, and I get reeled in by one of Grace's many good qualities again, just long enough to reevaluate my decision. The way we are together now is more like friends, anyway. And I want—so desperately—to remain friends with her. Because she knows me best. Because of how she listens to me with her head slanted and that small smile on her face, her glance all serious. And, mostly, because of how she can so easily put things in perspective for me due to her easy-going nature.

"When are you going to tell me what's going on with

you, Katie?" she asks, after having put her spoon to the side. She certainly hasn't grown less fond of bastardizing my given name, no matter what I tell her. Some people simply appear to have an inability to address their loved ones by their real name. A very normal sort of behavior according to Grace. She claims it increases intimacy between partners. Personally, I have no issues with simply calling her Grace.

Then her question sinks in. Is this my chance? Or will I chicken out again? Surely I can't tell her in a restaurant? That would be inhumane—much more so than actually breaking up with her.

I give her one of my trusted, sultry smiles. "I don't know," I lie. Because I have also considered that this might just be a bad patch between us—one of those things that every couple goes through—and that I would be giving up the love of my life. As soon as I start thinking in love-of-my-life terms though, I remember all the reasons why she isn't the one for me. "I just haven't been feeling myself lately." Later, when we get back to her apartment, I tell myself. "I don't really feel comfortable talking about it here." I glance around furtively to make my point. "Let's talk when we get home." Though, home is her place. Her tiny studio where we have to sleep half on top of each other because her bed is less than queen-sized—though still bigger than any bed in a dorm room.

"Okay." She gives me a nod with a grave expression on her face. "Because we need to talk."

It would be pretty naive of me to think that Grace hasn't caught on to my diminished amorous feelings for her. She's a smart girl, which is one of the reasons I fell for her in the first place. But, on the other hand, it's just so much easier to just continue with her. After almost a year together we have found our own rhythm, have made up a dialect of our own. It's the constant struggle between these two urges inside of me that is driving me mad.

"We do." I agree, because I'm starting to get sick of my

own voice when more lies come out of my mouth.

"Are you done?" She eyes my plate, which has remained largely untouched. My stomach is being occupied by a large ball of fear and nerves, leaving no room for food.

"Yeah. I'm not very hungry."

"I can see that." She sighs, and I take it as a sign of things to come. Maybe Grace will be the one stepping up in this situation. Maybe *she* will put *me* out of my misery. She starts looking around for a waiter, asks for the check.

When we get it, she pulls the piece of paper toward her, puts one hand on it, while she finds her wallet with her other.

This is one of the things about her that drive me insane. I don't want to be indebted to her. In the beginning, because I was falling in love, I let her pay for a meal a few times—always making certain I returned the favor promptly —but the economist in me only ever feels comfortable with going Dutch. She knows this. We have talked about this at length, which is why her doing this enrages me so much. Tonight, it feels like she's doing it on purpose.

"I'll pay for my share." I put a hand on hers, wanting to take the check from her.

"It's my treat tonight," she exclaims, deliberately antagonizing me—at least that's how it comes across to me.

"Why?"

"Do I need a reason to treat my girlfriend when she's feeling low?" Her voice sounds sweet enough, but there's something in her glance, something menacing—something that tells me she's more than up for a fight.

Without looking at the check, I dig a ten-dollar bill from my purse and put it on the table. Usually, I would pick the check apart and calculate exactly how much each of us owes. I slam the bill on the table. "I don't need to be treated. I can pay my own way."

"It's not about that." Grace is not backing down. "It's about you being able to accept me doing this for you. Why is it so hard?"

"Anything else you want to do for me, I will accept, just not this," I reply, trying to steal some deep breaths in between speaking, to calm myself down.

"That's a lie and you know it." Grace picks up my ten-dollar bill and waves it in my face. "Everything always needs to be exactly divided with you. The time we spend doing dishes and laundry. Hell, even the time we go down on each other." She narrows her eyes. "I'm sick of that, Katie."

"It's how I was brought up," I say, thrown by the rude comment she made and I can't help but examine my memory for instances of me timing cunnilingus. She is surely making that up to spite me. "The way I was raised, there was no other way."

"Maybe it's time you tried to change for the better then." The waiter has returned and she hands him her money, leaving mine on the table.

This is the time I shut down. I could, again, try to explain to her how disrespected her actions—and her words—make me feel, but when I reach a certain point of anger, no more words come out. The silent treatment it will be tonight. I wish her good luck with trying to have an adult conversation with me later.

Silently, each wrapped in our own displeasure, we leave the restaurant.

"I take it you don't want to go to Marcy's party anymore?" She's the first one to break the silence.

Marcy's party? Earlier, when Grace said we needed to talk tonight, I had interpreted that as neither one of us going to Marcy's party anymore.

"You go," I say. "I'm going home."

"Your home or my home?" She's starting to soften. So am I. When she looks at me like that, her eyes kind and her smile warm, I feel as though I'll never be able to break up with her.

"Yours," I acquiesce.

She steps closer to me. "Are you sure you don't want to come?"

I nod, but I make my nod seem reluctant. "I need some alone time." A phrase no considerate girlfriend can ever argue with.

"I love you," Grace says, and plants a soft kiss on my nose.

"Love you too." I smile, after which we both go our separate ways.

ALI

Anna was right. I do have feelings for Professor Julianne Seabolt. I probably shouldn't stay the night, though. It wouldn't be good for either of us.

"Will you give me an A plus?" I joke, while I run a finger over her belly. She's so pale. The dark color of my skin contrasts so deliciously with her light one.

"Talk to me in French and we'll see." Her face breaks out into a smile and it's as though I can feel it radiate through me.

"*S'il-vous-plaît*," I say in my heavily-accented French, still managing to sound like a native New Yorker. I wish I could speak it better, that Julianne's knowledge of the language would be transferred to me every time we had sex. I'd be fluent by now. We've gone from that smiley first kiss in her office to long sessions in her bed in a matter of weeks. I haven't slept with anyone else since. "*Je suis devenue monogame pour toi.*" And I have become monogamous for her.

She chuckles. "I'm honored, but I can't give you an A plus for that."

"Not even for extra effort?" My finger halts just below her breast.

"Is it that much effort?" She lifts up her head a little to

better look me in the eyes.

"Not really." It has been surprisingly easy, but she doesn't have to know that. We're not in the habit of explaining our personalities to each other.

"Is that what you want this to be? Monogamous?"

This makes my ears perk up. Does she mean she has been sleeping with other students? I push myself up and look her straight in the face. "This conversation is taking a turn for the absurd."

"Just for the record, I'm not sleeping with anyone else. I would consider that very… unsavory," she says.

"Unsavory, huh?" I glance down at her body and remember how she was spread open for me earlier, how she surrendered to my touch, and how much I enjoyed that. Because I am who I am, I wonder if this is my cue to walk away. But finals are still a few months away and I would have to sit through all those lectures with her, wondering if she had her sights set on anyone else in class, or if she missed me at all. Anna's words about her being in a position of power run through my head. I don't give that girl enough credit sometimes.

"Do we need to talk about this?" She runs a finger over my back and my skin breaks out in goosebumps. "We've been doing this for a while now. I understand if you have questions. I certainly have a few."

"Shoot." I go soft underneath her touch again, and I don't feel much like talking—I never do.

"What we're doing is against college rules, we both know that. Have you told anyone?" Her finger has stopped its caress.

"Only my best friend."

She drops her hand altogether and sits up with her back against the headboard. "You've actually told someone?"

"Anna is totally trustworthy. She won't tell anyone." Perhaps I shouldn't have told *her*.

"Anna Davis who takes French with you in my class?"

Her tone increases in pitch.

"Well, yeah… She came to me with a rumor and her being my best friend, I didn't deny it."

"Oh shit. This is bad, Alison. When did this happen?" Panic chokes her voice.

"A few weeks ago, but it's fine. Rumors like that are always going around. Trust me, nobody knows."

"What did Anna tell you exactly?" Julianne purses her thin lips together.

I exhale a deep breath. She's sucking all the fun right out of our affair. Though I do understand the position it puts her in. "Just that she'd heard you were involved with one of your students."

"And you didn't think to deny it? Did she mention you by name?"

"No, no, no. My name never came up. But I wouldn't worry about this too much. It sounds much worse than it actually is. You having an affair with a student was one of the first things I heard when I just started at NYU. It's just one of those persistent college myths, that's all."

"Is that why you came on to me?" Her demeanor seems to loosen up a bit. Surely she can't sit here and pretend to be innocent in all of this.

"Excuse me? *I* came on to *you*?" I'm both being coy and remembering how all I had to do was shoot her a suggestive smile to get an instant vibe of reciprocation back.

"Of course you did. You walked into my office all sultry and seductive. Mind you, nothing I haven't seen before from my students, but there was something different about you. Something I liked."

"Was it the fact that my grandfather funded most of the new library? That building must host a slew of French Lit books."

She cocks her head and gives me a confused look. "What are you insinuating?"

"Nothing. Nothing at all." We're naked in bed. This is

not a conversation I want to be having.

"Please don't feel as though you can't be honest with me, Alison." She speaks to me the way she would to any student in class.

"You may not know me very well, but if you did, you'd soon learn that I'm a very uncomplicated person. I have a few needs that I like to be met, that's all. I enjoy… this." I open my palms and let my hands drift through the air over the bed. "This is casual for me. I won't be asking you for any favors, nor will I blackmail you. That's not me. Moreover, your—our—secret is more than safe with me. And yes, I'm not going to lie, you have a bit of a reputation on campus, but please don't tell me you don't know about that, because that would make you look pretty stupid, which is something you're decidedly not. Let's just have a good time. I know I'm not the first student you've had in your bed, and I doubt I'll be the last."

A grin crosses her face. She stares at me intently for a few seconds, then says, "So this is just fun for you?"

"Of course it is. What else would it be?"

She shrugs, looks at me some more.

"Were you planning on asking for my hand in marriage?" I can't help but chuckle.

"What a wonderful hand that would be." She picks up my right hand and brings it to her mouth. She plants a kiss on it, then cuts her eyes back at me. "Fun it is, then."

When her lips find my mouth, I conclude that in all the time we've been doing this, this is the most profound conversation we've had. I'm not hoping for a repeat.

CHAPTER THREE

KATHERINE

If I don't do something, I won't get more than a C in French. I need to speak to Professor Seabolt and make her understand that my poor results are not because of lack of effort. All the time I fruitlessly put into mastering the French language is taking away from my focus on other courses. I'm not one to ask for special treatment of any kind, but I just want to make her understand that I made a mistake at the beginning of the year by enrolling in this course.

I sit on a bench outside the building that houses her office. Office hours are almost over. I clasp the last paper she graded between my hands, and my eyes lock on the comment she left in bright red marker in the top right corner: *sub par*. No teacher has ever described any of my work as sub par. Katherine Shepherd doesn't do sub par. Not even when I was dragged from country to country because of my father's military career, and I had to work much harder than any of my classmates to get the same grades, did I perform sub par.

The words are like a slap in my face. I need to talk to her. Something's stopping me, though. What will I say? Even worse, what if she makes me say it in French? I already feel so ill at ease with her, especially since at the last presentation I failed miserably at making myself sound even remotely French. Maybe it's because French is the language of love and I suck at love.

"Let it go," Grace said when I complained about the 'sub par' comment. "It's one course. Four credits. It will have zero effect on the rest of your life. Let it go now and become a happy person again."

I wish I could. I also wish I could have responded more kindly to her. Neither seem to be within the reach of my personality. My damned, wretched personality. Perfection was expected from me as soon as I was able to comprehend the term. I didn't have any brothers and sisters to share the burden of expectation with, either. Only hours of loneliness in yet another country, of which I could never sufficiently grasp the language either. If only my dad had been stationed in France, perhaps I would be better at it now. But the United States doesn't have a military base in France, and instead we got carted off to Germany, and the Philippines, and Japan.

I check my watch. It's one minute before five. It's now or never, because I know I won't come back tomorrow or the day after. This is the first time I've made it this far. If I don't hurry, her office will be closed. She must be a stickler for detail, judging from how painstakingly she corrects my French—though, rationally, I know she's only doing her job. I rush up the stairs and through the hallway, until I stand in front of her closed office door. Shit. Is she gone? Relief is already starting to wash over me, but there's another—more persistent—voice nagging me as well. *Nobody has ever called you sub par before.* I hear the soft murmur of voices coming from behind the door. A hushed chuckle. There's someone in there. It must be a fellow student. I take a deep breath and try to relax. I'll just wait until they come out. This won't take long.

I wait for ten minutes, but nobody exits the office. Professor Seabolt mustn't be such a stickler for detail after all, what with letting the other student stay past her office hours. This is good news for me, but the longer it takes for me to be let in, the bigger the chance of me fleeing at the last minute.

Another five minutes later, I'm tired of shifting my weight around in the hallway, and decide to try a knock on the door, just to let her know that someone is waiting outside. I rap my knuckles against the matted glass and wait. Standing closer to the door, I hear more muffled noises, another chuckle, and a sound I can't quite put my finger on. What on earth are they discussing in there? It must be in French, that's why it's not really getting through to me. I wait, but the door doesn't open. She must not have heard my knock, so I try again, a bit more forceful this time. I give it a polite ten seconds—even counting them in my head. Ten seconds during which my gaze locks firmly on the words 'sub par' on the paper in my hand again, and I feel the inadequacy run through me so fiercely that, by then, I have no problem opening the door unbidden.

At first, I can't see the professor, because she's hidden behind… another woman. Someone is straddling Professor Seabolt's lap. Am I seeing this right? Just as the penny drops, the woman turns around.

"Oh shit," she exclaims, and jumps up. Only then do I see Professor Seabolt, lipstick smeared all around her lips. I recognize the girl from my French class. Her name is Alison. She's annoyingly good. I now see why.

"I'm so sorry," I manage to exclaim after the first shock has subsided. "I knocked. Twice."

Professor Seabolt composes herself, though I can barely stand to look at her—and not just because of the smudged lipstick.

"Close the door, please, Katherine," she commands. She shoots Alison a cross look. I'm guessing it was her task to lock the door behind her when she came in.

I give the door a quick push and hear it fall shut.

From the back of my mind, an opportunity makes itself known. I also can't believe Professor Seabolt has the audacity to call me sub par while she's the one kissing students in her office.

"Obviously, you weren't meant to witness this, Katherine. I apologize." At least she doesn't insult my intelligence by claiming that 'it's not what I think'. "Can I help you with something?"

Perhaps the professor is getting a whiff of the smell of opportunity in the air as well.

"Can we talk in private?" I have no desire to start negotiations in front of a classmate.

"Of course." She nods at Alison, who, before exiting the room, gives me the most disdainful once-over. I can't believe the nerve of that girl. What does the professor see in her, anyway? Because she must see something if she's willing to risk her career for some fondling in her office—barely after hours.

Without being asked, I sit down across from her. As I do, I can't help but wonder what actions have taken place on this particular piece of furniture.

I'm ready to play the upper hand I so obviously have in this situation. "You gave me a C." My voice trembles a little. "I'm not claiming it's an unjust grade, but I'm really a straight A kind of student." My blood thumps in my veins. Am I really blackmailing my professor? But how can I possibly respect any comments she makes about my French when she goes and does something as immoral as frolick with her students?

"Can I count on your discretion?" She stares at me hard with those pale eyes of hers. It feels as though she's looking straight through me. "Because if I hear so much as a whisper of this on campus, I'll know where it will have come from, and your grades will plummet accordingly."

Wow. I would never have taken her for such an unethical creature. Not only is she accepting my blackmail, but she's protecting herself along the way. Though, I guess, she doesn't have much choice. She's not unethical *and* stupid.

Any respect I ever had for the professor is out the window now. I should, actually, take this to the Dean, because a human being like her shouldn't be allowed to teach young adults. But I have a C to deal with. Does this make me as bad as her?

"You can." The way I see it, I still—firmly—have the upper hand. Though I don't have actual tangible evidence, an accusation would be enough to destroy her. "I give you my word."

"Very well." Professor Seabolt busies herself with needlessly arranging some papers on her desk, then holds out her hand. "Give me your assignment. I'll have another look at it."

The word *thanks* almost rolls off my tongue automatically, but she doesn't deserve gratitude. Because I have to live with this from now on. I didn't come here for any of this. I just wanted to have an honest conversation. Instead I ended up making a sordid deal with the devil. Surely, I'm a victim of circumstances beyond my control, despite failing to do the right thing.

"I'll see you in class." I give her one more look, certain of the fact that from now on I'll always see her with lipstick smeared across her lips. Like a vulgar harlot. Then I leave her office, hoping I'll never have to set foot in it again.

ALI

I wait for the uptight girl outside the building. What did Julianne call her? Katherine or something? All I know about her is that she's terrible at French, and she knows it. In class, she's awfully self-conscious, not allowing the language to just take over, needlessly thinking about every word before she speaks it. I told Anna from the very beginning of the year. "That one will never speak French." But now she has something on Julianne and it's my fault.

Why didn't I lock the door? I don't even have to ask myself that question. It's for the same reason I forget to lock the front door of the house. Carelessness, my dad would call it. My mind always being on something else. I need to solve this, for Julianne. And for my parents, whom I don't want finding out about this from that stuffed-up prick, the Dean.

I hear footsteps approaching and brace myself for a confrontation.

"Hey," I scream, when she runs right past me. "Hold on."

She turns around. Her cheeks are flushed bright red. Then she gives me a smile I can't decipher.

"What does it take for you to keep your mouth shut?"

She raises her eyebrows. "You're bribing me?" Her voice is all superior.

"I'm just inquiring." Granted, I could have thought this through a bit more.

"What could you possibly have to offer me?"

Is she taking the bait? Engaging in this conversation is better than her rushing off without saying anything. But what do I have to offer her? "I'll do your French assignments until you graduate."

"No need." Her grin is so smug. She must have struck a deal with Julianne. The professor probably dealt with this already. She would have. Good, because I was about to offer this girl money. "Not that I would ever take anything from the despicable likes of you," she says, a lot of bite to her tone. She stands there shaking her head. "How can you even do that? Girls like you is what's wrong with the world."

"Excuse me?" I should just walk away. Let it go. But did she just stop short of calling me a whore?

"I don't understand how you can even consider sleeping with her. It's wrong on so many levels."

"That's absolutely none of your business." Not the best defense ever played, but it's all I've got.

"It takes all sorts, I guess." She says this with so much contempt in her voice, it spurs on my rage.

"Who are you to judge me? You don't know anything about me. You can shout from your moral high ground all you want but, as far as I know, you just struck a deal in there."

This gives her pause. When she doesn't immediately reply, I know I must have hit a sore spot. It's no surprise she's a goody-two-shoes. People like her are all over campus —making the rest of us look bad.

"I wouldn't want Professor Seabolt to ruin her career over… over someone like you," she spits. This is beginning to sound personal. Does she have something against me in particular, or just the kind of person I seem to represent to her? From where I'm standing, that kind of person looks like the exact opposite of her. Someone who actually enjoys college life. Perhaps a little too much at times, and with the wrong people, but I bet I have so much more fun than her.

She's probably going out with a nerd from the IT department. Has her life all figured out. Taking a French class is probably the most adventurous thing she's ever done. But I could stand here sizing her up all day, it won't help my case. Time to move on. Though her rude and sudden arrival at Julianne's office has robbed me of at least one orgasm.

"Think what you want of me and see if I care." I give her a ridiculous bow, just to mock her a little. Just because I can. "I shall now bid you and your uptightness adieu. Don't forget to live a little. You're only in college once." I tap two fingers against my forehead and turn around, even though I actually have to go in the direction she's standing in. I figure I have pushed things enough without shoving past her.

"Please don't ever act as though you know me," she says, but I pretend I didn't hear her. I'm very good at what I'm about to do next. Make myself believe this never happened. By the time I reach the bar where I'm supposed to meet Anna—three quarters of an hour early because of being rudely interrupted—I have forgotten all about Katherine or whatever her name is. After my second beer, I actually find it quite hot that Julianne managed to strike a deal with her so quickly. I make a few notes on a cocktail napkin. There's a song in there somewhere.

CHAPTER FOUR

KATHERINE

Maybe because of what I witnessed in Professor Seabolt's office, and how that dashed my world view a little bit, I finally break up with Grace.

As usual, we're having dinner at her place—rather disgusting cup noodles that I'll always associate with breaking up from now on—when, all of a sudden, she says, "I heard Seabolt is sleeping with someone in your French class. The one with the dreadlocks. I think she's called Alison West."

"I think we should break up," is my response. It's as much a reaction born from panic as from an overflowing bucket of negative emotions inside of me.

"What?" The chopsticks Grace is eating with freeze midway between her mouth and the cup.

"I'm sorry to blurt it out like that, but it's how I feel. How I've been feeling for a while."

Grace drops her chopsticks on the table, steaming noodles fanning out over the surface. "You're dumping me?"

By now, I've pictured many scenarios in my head about how this could play out. Knowing Grace, the most probable is a massive freak-out on her part. A reaction I would never be ready to deal with, regardless of how accurately I could predict it.

"Why?" She shoots up out of her chair. "Why are you

dumping me?"

"Gracie, please, calm down." For some reason, my brain then, inexplicably, decides to lapse into calling her Gracie. "It's not you, it's me." I have a dozen practiced clichés at the ready in my head. "It just hasn't been working for me anymore."

"But... I just booked that cabin in the Catskills." I hadn't expected her to be so practical about it.

"I thought you were going to wait?"

"Wait for what? For you to dump me?" The anger in her eyes feels like a punch in the gut.

"I'll pay for it. I'm sorry."

"Never mind the fucking cabin." She starts pacing around the tiny kitchenette. "How can we fix this?" She halts in front of me, a desperate, pleading look in her glance.

"Please sit down. I'll try to explain." Tears prickle behind my eyes. How am I going to explain this to her? "I love you, Grace. I really do, but more as a friend than a lover."

"A lover? What is this? The seventies?" She doesn't sit down, instead towers over me. "Fuck, Katie."

I witness how her initial anger deflates, see her crumble before my very eyes. Grace falling apart is, by far, the worst possible case scenario.

"Lately, we've been more friends than anything else. While on some level that works for me, it's hardly fair because of the expectations that come with a relationship."

"You mean sex." She sags into the chair she abandoned earlier.

"Not necessarily. Just how, er, we feel about each other."

"What? So you love me, but you're not *in* love with me?" Her voice drips with sarcasm.

"I just no longer believe we are right for each other." Breaking up with Grace is the hardest thing I've ever done in my life. Impatiently, I wait for a sense of relief to wash over me, but I only feel anguish at having to put her through this. Because what I said earlier is by no means a lie. I care greatly for Grace. I'm desperate for her to let me remain a part of her life, if not now, then at least later.

"Is there someone else?" Tears have started rolling from her eyes, but she doesn't attempt to catch them.

"No." I shake my head vigorously. "Look, Grace, you must have seen this coming at least a little… We weren't seeing eye-to-eye on so many things. The newness of the first months was fast wearing off."

"That doesn't mean we have to break up. That's how relationships work." She wipes some snot from her nose. From her tone I can deduce that she doesn't believe that herself.

"I tried. I really tried. I did my best to make it work. You are a wonderful woman. I'm absolutely certain you will make someone very happy some day. It's just not me. I'm too neurotic for you. I like rules too much. I would only curb your free spirit."

"But that's what I like about you so much. That you're so different."

Wrong words. What to say next? My best guess is the absolute truth. "I know it hurts, Grace. It hurts me too." I wring my hands together. "It hurts me much more than I believed it would."

"Then stay. We've been needing to have a talk like this for weeks. Just stay and we'll figure it out." She reaches for my hands, grabs them. Her fingers are wet with tears and snot. My first impulse is to pull my hands away, but this is not the time to give in to my germaphobia.

Slowly, I shake my head. "I can't. Deep down, you must know. You could be so much happier. Not immediately, but in the long run. Look at the future. In a few months, you will have graduated. You don't want to be tied down by your girlfriend who's still in college."

"I knew something was going on with you, but that

doesn't mean this doesn't feel like a knife's being planted straight into my heart. I love you, Katherine."

"I love you too, but it's not enough."

"Since when is love not enough?" She's still holding on to my hands, as though keeping them trapped in hers will prevent me from going through with this.

"It's not the right kind of love."

"Please don't tell me you want to be friends." She starts playing with my fingers, doesn't look me in the eyes.

I suspect now is not the right time to press for that. "I will be whatever you want me to be, Grace. Maybe it sounds foolish, but I want this to be as easy on you as possible. If you don't want to see me, I'll stay away. If you do, I'll be there. But I just really need you to see that none of this is your fault. You didn't do anything wrong. It's my loss, really."

"Stop… saying these things. Don't make me out like I'm some sort of saint." Finally, she lets go of my hands. "Maybe you should leave. Pick up your stuff some other time."

"Okay." Through the pain, the first signs of relief are starting to materialize. All things considered, she's letting me off easy. No big scenes. No massive melt-down, after all. She's graceful Grace as always. It's what I called her when we first met. *Would you hand me a paper towel, Graceful? And a spoon, please, Graceful?* She'd play along and pretend to be gliding over the floor, like Ginger Rogers when she was dancing with Fred Astaire. "Call me if you need me."

She just sits there mute, defeated. Maybe I'm just thinking this way to make myself feel better, but I know she'll soon realize this is for the best. Sometimes two people are better off not together.

I shuffle from one foot to another, not sure if a hug would be extremely inappropriate, or exactly what she wants right now. Awkwardly, I scoot forward and throw my arms around her. She remains immobile in my embrace, so I let go.

ALI

"It has simply become too dangerous," Julianne says. "You must realize that. I can't open myself up to any more blackmail. If we end it now, we destroy all proof."

I'm not used to being on the receiving end of a break-up conversation. Despite my twenty years of age, I've made many a heartfelt dumping-speech already, and this feels like a feather is being plucked forcefully from my cap. And all because of that spindly girl with her blond hair pinned tightly to her head who came barging into Julianne's office—a place I've been banned from ever since. Though she seems like the type who would always sit at the front of any classroom, in Julianne's French class she keeps to the back. Last week I positioned myself to the side of the auditorium so I could keep an eye on her. Not even Little Miss Perfect could pretend she wasn't just there for appearance's sake. From what Julianne has told me, she doesn't need to come to class anymore. Her final grade has been determined already.

"We can't continue tempting fate like that."

"You know what you should do?" I change the subject because I categorically refuse to hear what Julianne is saying. "You should let that bitch who caught us believe that you're going along with her scheme, but when push comes to shove, give her a fucking F on her finals. We'll see who has the last laugh then."

"Ali, come here." Julianne opens her arms wide. I just stare at them, not moving an inch. "Meet me halfway here." She takes a few steps in my direction. I cross my arms in front of my chest, lest she try to grab for my hands, and take them into hers. "You must have known this couldn't last. Didn't you say this was just fun?"

"It's not so much fun now."

She puts her hands on my shoulders. I don't shrug them off. Maybe it's the last time she'll ever touch me. "I know it's not. I'm sorry," she says.

"I get it, but I'm not happy about it. I love fucking you. You're so completely different than any of the girls I've slept with before. I don't feel much like going back to that. Twisted as it may be, I liked what we had. A lot. It gave me a weird sense of purpose. Like there was more to college than sleeping around, you know?" I pull up my shoulders. "I don't know."

She takes another step closer, her face dangerously close to mine. "I know."

"I'm only a junior, I have one more year to go. What if I feel sad every time our paths cross?" I slant my head. Give her *the look*.

"Then know that I will feel sad also." She leans in but, instead of kissing me on the lips, she pecks me lightly on the nose.

I'm not sure if I feel sad or angry or just enormously deflated. But she is right. It would have been supremely foolish of me to have expected this affair to go on and on. It already lasted way past any of my previous relationships, if you can even call them that. I also refuse to have my heart even the slightest bit broken by my professor. What kind of a cliché would that make me? At tomorrow's gig, I'll just look extra sultry, sing the low notes extra low, and drive some girls crazy. I harnessed my talent years ago and have gotten very skilled at employing it to my advantage.

"Are you going to replace me?" I can't just shuffle off without giving her any lip. It's not my style. "I asked around and the girl who has your fate in her hands is a lesbian, has a proper girlfriend and everything. Maybe that would be a way to shut her up for good."

Julianne intensifies her grip on my shoulders. "Ali, you're a sweet girl underneath it all, but your mouth is way too big for your own good."

This time I do shrug her hands off me. "Why do you do it, anyway? Fuck your students? All that risk for what? The feel of a young breast in your hand? It's a little"—I remember the word she used once—"unsavory, isn't it?"

"Please, don't be like that. We had a good time together, didn't we? Let's not spoil the beautiful memories we made by being crass." She shuffles backwards. "That being said, it's understandable that you would be upset."

"I'm not upset, I'm just curious. Someone as accomplished and good-looking as you could have any woman. Why fool around with your students? Because I assume I wasn't your first."

"I think it better to not give too much thought to the why," is all she says. Was I really expecting her to bare her soul to me? Some women prefer to be completely naked with someone else instead of letting another human being glimpse into their soul. I'm one of them, so I back off.

"Well, then, Julianne Seabolt, it was nice knowing you… intimately." Damn it. I'm actually going to miss her.

"I'll see you in class." She pins her gaze on me.

"Hm. Somehow I'm not so sure of that. I hope my grades won't suffer if I were to be inconvenienced for the remaining lessons and couldn't make it to your lectures anymore."

She gives a cynical chuckle.

I decide to play it up a little. "Beneath that big mouth of mine, hides a sensitive heart." I tap my chest for effect.

"Okay. Deal." Julianne is nothing if not pragmatic, and willing to sacrifice the last of her integrity to save her own skin.

"Bye, Julianne." I let her name roll off my tongue slowly, then scrunch my lips together while I give her one last good look. Already, I'm jealous of the next junior she'll get her claws into. I walk over to her and kiss her on the cheek, inhaling her scent one last time. Then I'm out the door.

I'd be lying if I said it didn't hurt a little bit. Damn you, Katherine Shepherd—I looked up her name. Damn you to hell and back.

CHAPTER FIVE

KATHERINE

Oh shit. It's her. I slow my step as I see her long dreadlocks bop up and down as she walks. I hope she's not going to the library. I really don't feel like another blow-out like the one she instigated outside of Professor Seabolt's office that day I walked in on them.

She has the sort of springy walk of the overly confident. Her knees bend too much. It's silly. Is that why the professor stooped so low? Because of her easy confidence?

I'm so lost in thought, there are only a few yards between us left, so I make myself slow down. There's a bench coming up around the bend and I'll just wait there until she's out of sight. I prefer to be reminded of what I saw that day as little as possible. Not that it was hugely traumatizing, just unsettling because of course you hear about things like that happening, but witnessing it with your very own eyes is a different thing entirely.

I stand still for a minute, actually waiting for the big arrow to move on my watch, then continue walking again. The library is big enough for both of us—and I doubt I'll find her in the economics aisle. I don't know what she majors in, but my best guess is that she's getting her MFA. She looks like the type.

As soon as I round the bend and glance at the bench

I've chosen to wait at, I see it's occupied. By her. I look away quickly, straighten my posture and hurry past it, hoping she hasn't spotted me.

"Hey. You," I hear from behind my back.

Involuntarily, I flinch. It's a minute reaction, but she must have noticed, because next she says, "Yes, *you*, Shepherd!" I do hope she's not going to make a scene again.

I take a deep breath and turn around. It's an early spring day and she's dressed in just a V-neck t-shirt. She must be very warm-blooded, because I'm still wearing my winter coat. Or maybe she just had a very warming meeting with Professor Seabolt.

"What?" I put as much hostility in my voice as I can muster. Faced with Alison West, that appears to be a lot.

"I hope you're happy now." She places her elbows on the bench and leans back, as though engaging in casual conversation with me.

"Why would I be happy?" I'm definitely confused. Is she referring to my blackmail situation? Although I prefer to think of it as that one time in my life I was really thinking on my feet and made the most out of a bad situation.

"She dumped me, so you can get off your high horse now. It's all over thanks to you."

My mouth droops open. This girl is just beyond belief. Thanks to me? "The way I see it, I've done you a huge favor. She was obviously taking advantage of you." I speak in hushed tones. We are in a public space and plenty of students are walking past.

Alison shakes her head. "There you go with your unfounded judgments again. You think you know everything, but let me tell you something; you don't."

"Oh really? So you were going to walk off into the sunset with her, were you?" I take a moment to shoot her a disdainful look. "Well, I guess you do deserve each other, both being amoral, despicable creatures and all that."

If Alison is offended by what I just said, she doesn't

show it. She just chuckles, which enrages me even more. She looks at me from under her long lashes. I kind of get what Professor Seabolt must have seen in her. She has something very seductive about herself. But damn it, that doesn't mean that the things that happened should have.

"What do you care, anyway, Shepherd?"

"I don't." My voice goes high-pitched. "You're the one who called me over. I want nothing to do with you."

"Just lighten up, okay? It's all over." She bends towards me and lowers her voice. "You'll have your straight As at the end of the year. Everybody's happy."

What does she mean *lighten up*? And where does she get the nerve to speak to me the way she does? There's something about her that rubs me up the wrong way. Maybe the fact that she doesn't want to admit to the mistake *she* made. "Just for the record, I didn't mean to run in on you. Nothing that has happened to you is my fault. I knocked. Multiple times!"

"All right, all right." She holds up her hands. "You're completely innocent. Go about the rest of your life guilt-free. Aspire for perfectionism all you can, even if you have to blackmail one or two more people along the way. I wish you the very best." The smirk she paints on her face is infuriating. She's accusing *me* of being without scruples now? One side of me wants to desperately continue to give her a piece of my mind, while the other, more sane part, knows I need to walk away from this pointless conversation.

"Whatever." I shrug, hoping it will have the same effect on her as her doing it would have on me. I give her one last look and head to the library.

"That's the spirit, Shepherd," she yells after me, and I can hear the contemptuous chuckle in her voice.

When I reach the library, my eyes catching the inscription above the entrance, I pause. The West Library. Isn't Alison's last name West? It would figure. She's just a spoiled rich girl treating college like her playground to do whatever the hell she pleases.

I glance from the sign to the bench behind me. She's still sitting there as though she doesn't have a care in the world.

ALI

I'm not feeling it tonight. The vibe in this bar is off. Too many loud frat boys in the back. Though the girl who's been eyeing me from the side from the very first song of my set is making me feel a little better. I glance at her, then exchange a meaningful look with Jennifer. Maybe we should have a threesome tonight. I don't know. Ever since Julianne ditched me, I haven't felt like being alone in a room with another girl. I finish the song and thank the few people who applaud me. One of them is Anna, of course. She brought a girl with her and they've been frolicking a lot, even during "Anna Begins" which I always sing especially for her. But I'm happy for her. Jennifer won't be too pleased though.

"One more," I whisper to Jen.

She nods and plays the first chord of the song I always close my set with. "Lilac Wine" it is. I could do with some wine, lilac or not, myself after this gig.

I decide to drown out my surroundings and just go for it. To just pour my soul into the delivery of this song. Just sing and forget about everything else. Only on stage can I feel this free. It isn't about the attention, but about being able to express myself in the purest way I know. Just me, my voice and a microphone.

This is something Jennifer and I theorize about a lot. Something I've tried to explain to Anna many a time. Not that she doesn't get it, but I truly believe you can only fully understand when you take to the stage yourself and experience what it's like to be up here. To sing—or play guitar in Jennifer's case—your heart out and fill the room with sounds that wouldn't exist if we weren't producing them. To Jennifer and me, music is the one true language. The ultimate form of inner expression. It's a way of life. A way that has garnered us our fair share of female—and male —attention. To Anna's great dismay. At least she was glad to hear that my affair with Julianne had ended.

I hold a note at the top of my voice while I think about Professor Julianne Seabolt. She was something special, I can see that now. I'm not the type to go back and beg for seconds, but that doesn't mean that, in the deepest recesses of my brain, I haven't considered it. I'm adamant to break the spell tonight—my post-Julianne dry spell. I've come to the last chorus and glance at the blonde again. She will more than suffice.

After the song is done, Jennifer gets up from her bar stool and, hand-in-hand, we bow to the small crowd together. I hold the blonde's gaze when I do, then give Anna a quick appreciative tilt of the head. I feel over the moon to have my two main girls with me here tonight. They always make me feel a bit better about myself.

After heading off the stage I go straight to the bar and order a beer for myself and the blonde. Maybe she will turn out to be the one. Who knows? Yeah right.

I shuffle up to her, hand her the beer, my fingers lingering, and say, "I'll be right back." Vain as it may sound, sometimes I think I have it too easy. All it seems I have to do is get up on stage and sing a few tunes. An acceptable singing voice appears to be a very potent aphrodisiac for lesbian NYU students.

"That was awesome," Anna's date says. She holds up a fist for me to bump mine against. Really? I give her a slow nod and a fist bump nonetheless.

"Do you have some business to attend to?" Anna asks, as she rolls her eyes at me. My best friend knows me all too well.

"It appears I do." I sling an arm around her shoulders and pull her to me.

"Would you not rather have an intellectual conversation with Mona and me?" She looks at me the way she always does at this point. Not quite disapproving, but not exactly accepting either. Sometimes I have no clue why Anna and I are friends, but then I look into her kind face, and catch a glimpse of that easy smile she has, and I remember. By now, this is more of a game we play, anyway. It's not because Anna is the opposite of a one-night stand girl that she begrudges me getting my kicks the way I see fit.

"What do you want to talk about?" I take a sip from my beer and, from the corner of my eye, sneak a glance at the blonde.

"Just go," Anna says, apparently not in the mood to tease me for much longer. Or maybe she wants me away from her table before Jennifer joins us. My two best friends will never see eye to eye, but I'm not the kind of person who needs them to.

I nod at her and make my way to the blonde, hand outstretched. "Hi, I'm Ali," I say.

"So am I," she says.

"It's a popular name." I give her a smile and hold up my bottle so we can clink the necks together. "Only given to the best among us."

"Hear, hear." She gazes deep into my eyes and encroaches on my personal space a bit—not that I'm a stickler for keeping my distance during flirting. But Blonde Ali is very much in my face from the beginning, making me believe this isn't going to be much of a challenge. Good. I don't feel much like working hard for it tonight. "You're really good," she says, which always makes me feel a bit awkward, despite having been showered with compliments from a very young age. Being the youngest of four children will do that to you.

"Thank you." Should I make my move already? I

haven't come to her table for a deep conversation either. "Do you live around these parts?"

I could easily have moved out of my parents' house when I started college, just like my siblings did when their time came, but ever since my last-remaining sister left the house four years ago, I've enjoyed the space she left me with. And I know Mom likes having me around still. I was never going to move into a dorm room, and it just seemed like such a waste to get my own apartment. It helps that I have a hot meal waiting for me at home whenever I want it and that I don't have to do my own laundry. But I don't treat our house like a hotel where I can just freely take girls up to my room. Maybe, one day, if I'm serious enough about a girl, I'll take her home, but not tonight.

Blonde Ali proceeds to tell me all about where she lives, what she's majoring in, where she's from, and I listen patiently, until I ask, "Shall we get out of here then?"

And then we do.

PART TWO

2002

CHAPTER SIX

KATHERINE

I'm hunched over my computer screen—the company just invested in brand new flat screen monitors for everyone—studying a spreadsheet, when my phone rings. It's past eight o'clock on a Friday evening. There's only one person who would call me at work now.

"I knew it, Kat," Grace says. "I demand you stop what you're doing at once and join me for a drink." These days, it doesn't wind me up so much anymore when she calls me Kat.

"You don't pay my salary, so you really have no say in the matter." I stretch my back as I cradle the receiver between my head and shoulder. I've been sitting for way too long.

"It was a long shot to get you out tonight, but tomorrow you're coming out with me. I need you to promise me now."

I sigh, although I could do with a night out. I also haven't seen Grace, my best friend, in way too long. "Where do you want to go?"

"There's a new lesbian bar just around the corner from our place. Come over. Stay the night. Or not, if you get lucky." She giggles into the phone. "We'll hang out on Sunday. Just relax. Anything to take your mind off work."

"Does Sandra have the weekend shift again?" I ask,

jokingly.

"She does, not that that has anything to do with it."

"I was just kidding, Grace. Why so testy?"

"No reason. I'm sorry. She's been working a lot of weekend and night shifts lately. I don't get to see enough of her."

"Don't worry. I'll be at your front door with an overnight bag tomorrow afternoon. We'll have a good time. I promise."

"Thanks, Kat." Grace's tone lightens up. "Now also promise me that after you hang up you'll shut down your computer and go home. Felix must be waiting for you."

"I promise," I say in a whiny voice, though I know I'll stay for at least another hour.

"I know you won't, but I hope I at least made you feel a little guilty about it." Grace knows me too well.

"I'll see you tomorrow." I end the conversation and hang up. My mind drifts to Felix. He's probably snoozing on my bed right now, oblivious to the fact that I'm not there. When I first got him, I had hoped he'd be an affectionate pet, but he hid underneath the couch for at least three days, and in all the years I've had him I've rarely heard him purr. Then my glance meanders to the only picture frame on my desk. It's one of Grace and me on her graduation day, one year before mine. We'd only just become friends again, long after I'd given up hope that we ever would. But here we are, six years after I felt compelled to break up with her—a decision I never regretted although I missed her terribly in the beginning. And she found love again. She and Sandra have been shacked up together in Brooklyn for a few years now.

My own love life hasn't fared so well. Grace sometimes jokes that if even she wasn't good enough for me, which other mere mortal could ever be good enough for Katherine Shepherd? But I don't consider myself that difficult, though it doesn't help that I've been living alone since I left my

NYU dorm room, and I have become set in my own ways.

I try to refocus on the spreadsheet, but the numbers start dancing in front of my eyes. I bargain with myself that if I go home now and come in for two to three hours tomorrow morning, this report will be done before Monday. After all, I moved only two blocks away from the office for a reason.

I stretch my back again, rub my eyes and power down my computer. Perhaps Grace has more influence over me than I believe. When I leave my office, which I got two years before anyone else who started at Powell & Cooper at the same time as I did, I notice that I'm not the only one working late on a Friday night.

"We're definitely not a company that adheres to the nine-to-five schedule," I was told when I interviewed for the job as a junior analyst. Truer words were never spoken. Twelve-hour days are more the norm than the exception. No wonder my love life has been suffering. But, after graduation, I had no issue putting my career first. What else was I going to do? Marry rich, have babies and waste my college education? I don't think so.

On my way to the elevator, my stomach growls, which elicits a deep sigh. It would be so easy to pick up a few slices of pizza on the way home, but I insist on cooking myself a healthy meal every evening. How else am I going to keep up this pace? I'm sure Grace has foreseen a plethora of unhealthy snacks—and cocktails—for us tomorrow evening. I love her dearly, but she's a prime example of what I've seen lesbian coupledom do to women's waistlines. They just stop caring and eat whatever they want, as though once they've found a mate, their health stops mattering. I've tried to talk to her about the risks of a protruding belly, but Grace waved me off and simply said, "Stop judging."

"I'm not judging," I said. "I care for you and your health."

"Sandra's a nurse," she replied. "Do you think you

know better than her?"

They've been together for almost four years, and I do envy them sometimes. What's more important? Being able to buy the same size jeans every year or coming home to a long-term partner every evening?

As I walk the two blocks to my apartment I consider that, perhaps, I'd be willing to have a bucket of KFC once in a while if it got me a steady girlfriend.

ALI

It's not often I can make it to one of Mom's Friday evening dinners, but tonight I have no plans. I have a gig tomorrow, but tonight I'm free as a bird. Free to sit through a meal with my lawyer father, my cardiologist mother, my two lawyer sisters and my oncologist brother. If it weren't for me, my parents could actually consider the family they raised as picture perfect.

They would never say it out loud, of course, because I'm little Ali, their youngest, their artistic, creative girl. But it doesn't mean I can't sense it, especially at one of these dinners, when my eldest sister Bianca's flawless children will be there as well, along with her perfectly-matched husband —star Manhattan Assistant District Attorney and on track to either launch a political career or get poached by one of New York's top law firms. I have a hunch he'll go for the money in the end. Not that anyone in my family needs more of that.

A few weeks ago, my brother Clayton's wife Denise invited me to lunch at a posh place on the Upper East Side, and had the audacity to ask me, in unveiled terms, when I was going to start doing something with my life. Typical Clayton to let his wife do his dirty work. When I pointed out to Denise that she doesn't have a job, she said, "I have the most important job of all, Ali. I'm a mother-to-be and a homemaker."

My eyes nearly rolled out of my head.

"I *am* working on my career," I said. "One gig at a time."

Denise nodded, then said, "You sure have done a lot of gigs, but I see no evidence of a career."

It's not really like me to burst out of a restaurant in an offended fashion, but, maybe for the first time in my life, I felt like doing so. Because who is she to talk to me like that? Yes, we are the same age, but we are nothing alike. I never even particularly liked her. She's way too stuffy. An opinion I freely shared with Clayton before he asked her to marry him. As usual, he ignored me. And then he has her speak to me like that?

Last I heard, Denise is eight and a half months pregnant, so perhaps she won't be at dinner tonight. Though chances are she will be, because it would be a perfect opportunity to draw attention to herself and explain to us silly Wests why it is so important to be a stay-at-home mom. My mother never was, nor is Bianca. My other sister, Nessa, to whom I'm the closest in age, has had a boyfriend for years, although she doesn't seem to be very interested in marrying him. But she's a lawyer, so it doesn't matter to anyone what she does in her private life. She's focusing on her career the way it should be done. Not the way I'm doing it—another thing they would never say, but I hear in the silences that fall when the subject of me singing for a living comes up.

I walk from my loft in Chelsea to Park Avenue. It's not a short trek, but I need it to clear my head. To center myself before facing them. Sometimes, on these walks over, I fantasize about arriving at my parents' house and once and for all telling them how I feel. They'd all be sitting in the lounge having manhattans or a tiny glass of sherry—or filtered water with a hint of ginger for Denise—and look at me as I enter, and I would shout, "Is money really so much more important than happiness?" But I'm long past saying that. It wouldn't make any difference and they would just judge me even more, and argue and argue—debate, as my dad likes to call it. I never seem to be in the mood for one of his debates.

I'm so different from my siblings, I have wondered where the deviation in genes has come from. Physically, we look alike enough, though they all dress much too old for their age, but character-wise, we're worlds apart. Unless they all have hidden ambitions and have just found a way to suppress their creative needs. But me, I can't imagine a life without singing. I need to be on the stage several nights a week, no matter how little it pays.

"But don't you want to be independent?" Nessa asked me a while back. "Does it not make you uncomfortable to live off Mom and Dad's money?"

I just shrugged, because the fact of the matter is that it does the exact opposite. It makes me feel comfortable to know I don't *have* to sing for money. I wasn't raised too spoiled, though I did have it good. But I was never made to feel guilty about accepting money either. It's just there. It always has been. Why wouldn't I use it?

The way I see it, they're all over-achievers and I'm the normal one. I don't have grand expectations for my life. I just want to do my own thing. Sing. Be happy. Be free.

I've almost arrived and, automatically, I slow my pace. But, in the end, they may all be judgmental creatures, they're also my family, and I love them.

After kissing Mom hello in the kitchen—she insists on preparing one meal a week herself for her offspring—I head into the lounge and only see my dad, my brother and my sisters. Nessa's boyfriend Eric, who is a homicide detective, usually doesn't make it to these shindigs, so I'm not surprised he's not present. But Bianca's husband isn't there either and neither is Denise. It must be my lucky night then.

It's always easier to be the only single person in the room when my siblings' significant others aren't present.

CHAPTER SEVEN

KATHERINE

The bar Grace has taken me to is called Temptation, though we've been here for more than an hour and I haven't seen anything tempting. Grace is drinking a highly calorific cocktail, while I stick to Pinot Grigio.

"I know this is not the best place to bring this up," Grace says, "but I think Sandra might be cheating on me."

"What?" I nearly knock over my wine glass. "Why do you think so?"

"A woman knows, you know? And her shifts seem to be getting longer and longer as time progresses. When I dare to ask about that, she gets all defensive. Says that she'd like to be head nurse one day. But I don't buy it."

"Jesus, Grace. I hope it's not true." In situations like these, I'm the worst friend. I have no clue what to say. Over the years that they've been together, Sandra has become my friend as well, though I don't see nearly as much of her, what with her shift work and all.

"I'm not a hundred percent sure, but what can I do? Follow her to the hospital? And what if I accuse her and I'm wrong?"

I stare into my now empty wine glass, then look at Grace. Her usually sparkly brown eyes have gone all dull. "You can't live with that kind of uncertainty. You need to do something."

"I know." She nods slowly. "But right now, I'm just going to have another martini." She looks around for a waitress—thank goodness this is not one of those places where you have to make your way through a throng of people you don't know to order at the bar.

We place our order for another round, which gives me time to come up with some best-friend advice. "Would you like me to talk to her?" I ask.

Grace doesn't have time to ponder my question and reply, because on the small stage in the corner of the bar one of the bartenders has taken the mic.

"We have an extra temptation for you tonight, ladies," she says. "Please put your hands together for the amazing Ali West."

"There's entertainment?" I ask, not sure if I feel like sitting through a loud concert, especially now that Grace has shared her suspicions about Sandra with me. "Do you want to leave?"

"We just ordered drinks," she says. "And maybe's she's good." She turns to look at the stage and I do the same.

Although the name Ali West didn't register, I recognize her instantly. It's her. The girl from college who slept with my French professor.

"Hello, Brooklyn," she says into the microphone. "I shall sing you a few songs." She tilts her head as though saluting the audience and nods at the woman next to her holding a guitar. "This one's called "Free Me" and I wrote it myself. Don't worry, I'll sing a few covers later. Might even throw in a bit of Tracy Chapman."

The crowd responds with a few claps and encouraging howls. The music starts and she sways to the melody a bit, then grabs the mic with both hands and begins to sing.

"I know her," I whisper to Grace. "We were in French class together in college. She's the one who, you know…"

"Who what?" she asks. "Christ, she's hot. Are you finally feeling tempted, Kat?"

"No way. She's the one who had the affair with Professor Seabolt."

"So, she's a member of the big rainbow family then." Grace quirks up her eyebrows. "Yum."

I'm guessing the martinis she's been knocking back in quick succession are starting to take away her inhibitions.

"I'm telling you, Pussycat. If Sandra leaves me…" She doesn't finish her sentence, probably realizing the heftiness of her supposition. Then the audience starts clapping. Ali has finished her first song. "Just shut up for a minute, okay, Kat? I want to listen to the next one." Grace turns away from me, facing the stage, a fresh cocktail in her hand. "Woohoo," she shouts.

Ali's next song is a cover version of "Constant Craving"—she clearly knows her audience—and I have to admit that she sings it well. Her voice is very dynamic and she already has a few ladies in front of the stage entranced. She basically still looks the same as she did in college. Her hair is still braided into dreadlocks. Her clothes are certainly nothing I would still wear, but I guess the rules are different for someone like her.

College seems so long ago. Long days at work have erased the memory of those, in hindsight, rather carefree years—though they were never really carefree for me. That incident in Professor Seabolt's office feels like a lifetime ago. Still, I do remember. I remember the false grade it yielded me in French, a language I forgot as soon as I graduated. Does Alison still speak it?

The crowd is going wild on the very low notes and, oh, Ali West is very good at batting her lashes. Grace seems enthralled. Does she do this for a living? Sing in lesbian bars on weekends? I hope it's just a hobby because it can't bring in much.

"Thank you so much, ladies. You're too kind," Ali says after she finishes the song. She asks for a round of applause for the woman playing guitar. "My best friend Jen has come out for the occasion," she says. "She wanted to see what Temptation was all about. It's pretty awesome." She does that tilt of the head again. "You may recognize the next one."

She doesn't say what it is and I don't recognize it, but I've never been much into music. I look at her and wonder if she's still so annoying. I remember her getting right under my skin in no time back in the day. Maybe I'll find out tonight.

ALI

"If it isn't Katherine Shepherd." In my job, I see familiar faces in the crowd all the time. I don't always say hello, but I have to say hello to Shepherd. Just to amuse myself a little. Though the gig was a hoot already. A female crowd isn't always easy, but once you manage to snare their attention, you have it unequivocally for the rest of the night. I even threw in some requests near the end, which always gains me sympathy.

"Alison. Wow," Shepherd says. "You haven't changed a bit."

She certainly has. She's dressed in a white blouse, with only one button open at the collar, and a black cardigan. I don't think she's a regular in the bar scene. "I'll take it as a compliment."

"You are so good up there," Katherine's friend—or maybe it's her partner?—says.

"This is my friend Grace, who also went to NYU," Katherine says.

We exchange some pleasantries—Grace seems to have really enjoyed my gig—and then I look Katherine straight in the face and ask, "How's your French these days?" It's just a joke, a way to gauge how she has evolved over the years.

"Funny you should bring that up," she says, and, I might be wrong because it's pretty dark in the bar, but a mild blush creeps from her neck to her cheeks. "I can hardly proclaim to be fluent in it."

"I've forgotten all of mine," I say, happy to know we've all moved on. She must still be a lesbian, though, otherwise she wouldn't be here. "I lost my incentive to work at it so…"

"Do you perform often?" Shepherd asks. Maybe it's rude to address her by her last name, even if it's only in my head, but it's how my mind refers to her.

"As often as I can." Always on the look-out for new opportunities, I slip my hand in my back pocket and take out two business cards. I hand one to each of them. "Do give me a buzz if you'd like me to play for you some day."

Shepherd stares at the card, as though some hidden truth is buried in the small black letters on it, while her friend Grace says, "You can come play for me at my house any time. I live just around the corner."

I don't remember her from college. Maybe she was a late bloomer, or maybe Jen knows her. Jen isn't my regular guitar player anymore, she has a wife, a child and a dog now, but she was more than happy to replace Barry for the occasion. "I don't do house calls, but if I did, it would be my pleasure." I shoot her a smile. The way she's swaying on her bar stool, she looks pretty far gone.

"Nice to meet you, Grace. Good to see you again, Katherine." I tap two fingers against my forehead and say my goodbyes. As I make my way to Jen, I nod at a few more people, but avoid conversation. Seeing Shepherd has made me think of Julianne. It stung when she ended it, but I got over that a long time ago.

"Remember when things blew up with Seabolt?" I say to Jen. "She's the one who walked in on us." I point to Shepherd and see her staring straight at me. Ghosts from the past will have that effect on you. Additionally, despite her grandma-clothing—that's actually how my own grandmother dresses—she's the hottest chick here tonight. A few extra years have made her cheekbones stand out more and she has a strangely sultry look about her, like she's actively fighting the passion inside of her.

"Great possible point of entry," Jen jokes.

"It's you and me tonight, buddy." I ask the bartender for two beers. "For old times' sake."

"I wouldn't want to come in between you and a conquest." Jen sits down next to me. "I know how much you like a challenge."

"Don't you miss it?" I turn to face her. "Now that you've been on stage with me for a full set for the first time in more than five years… how do you feel?"

"Glorious as it was, I'm a different person now."

It's true. She is. She couldn't be further removed from the Jennifer I knew in college. Anna would actually be interested in her now. Though Anna is doing her own shacking up somewhere in New Jersey. We're in touch, but not as much as I'd like to be. Our lives are oceans apart. My life especially seems to be so different from everyone I went to college with. But this is New York, where it's easy to make new friends, and where you can always find a place where you belong. "Don't tell me you miss your wife already?" I joke.

Jen shoots me a grin. "Not a chance. Not tonight." She holds up her bottle, then knocks most of its liquid back in one go.

I like a good time, but I prefer to pace myself when I drink. Some nights I don't go on stage until well past midnight and I have enough pride in my work not to do so intoxicated. But tonight, my work is done. I'm in a lesbian bar. All I have to do is swivel around on my bar stool and the party can begin. Though it's not the same as it was in college. When you've lost count of the number of women you've slept with, it becomes less important to add yet another. I'm not in it for the conquest anymore. Though, in my profession, it's hard to find someone to settle down with.

★ ★ ★

Two hours and many beers later, Shepherd is still there. I've sneaked glances at her and she and her friend seemed to be engaged in a very lively conversation. At one point, Shepherd even threw her arms around Grace, as though she was comforting her. They're still sitting at the same table. The crowd has thinned. Next to me, Jen is so wasted, she slouches in her seat and her head keeps falling forward. She's not used to this anymore.

I turn to the bartender and ask her to bring Shepherd and her friend a round of drinks from me. I wait until they've been delivered, then head over.

"I need to go to the bathroom," Grace slurs. "Please excuse me." She waddles away.

"Thanks for the drinks, though Grace really didn't need another one." Shepherd holds up her wine glass.

"You're still here. I thought that needed to be celebrated." I'm hardly still sober myself but, over the years, I've learned to drink plenty of water in between alcoholic beverages.

"I've been trying to get her to go home for more than an hour, but it seems my powers of persuasion are less effective than alcohol. She's going through a bit of a tough time."

"Ah, lady trouble?" I drag a stool from a nearby table and sit down.

"Something like that." Shepherd scans the bar for a sign of Grace returning. "I hope she's all right in there."

"Give her a few minutes." I do my head slant and give Shepherd a look from under my lashes. Jennifer hit the nail on the head earlier when she said I liked a challenge. Seducing a girl who I once outraged with my actions would be the ultimate challenge. It's late. I'm single. The first thing I need to do is find out if she is, then gauge her interest. "It's nice to see you again, Katherine, though we never did get off on the right foot."

She snickers. "You can say that again." She cuts her eyes at me, looks into mine briefly. "Though I think I've gotten over our dramatic first encounter by now."

"Good." I sink my teeth into my bottom lip, trying to find her gaze again. I'm starting to get fired up. "Maybe we can start again."

"Maybe." As soon as Katherine's glance finds mine, she averts it. Maybe this is how she flirts. Maybe insecurity is her game. Or maybe she simply has no clue of what she's doing and this is just a friendly conversation to her. In essence, it is.

"I'd like that." I lean my elbows on the table and scoot a little closer, invading her space a bit, letting my intentions be known. It's too late at night for subtlety.

"Ali, er, are you—" she starts to say, then looks away.

"I think I need to go home." Grace has made her way back to the table at the worst possible time. "Everything is spinning."

Katherine rushes to her feet and holds her by the elbow. "Sorry about that." She gives a nervous chuckle. "We need to go."

I open my palms and nod. "I get it."

"Thanks for the drinks," she repeats.

"You have my number." I mime the universal telephone sign. "Call me." I watch as they leave, and I know that Katherine Shepherd is never going to call me.

I collect Jen from her dozing position at the bar and take her home before returning to my own empty bed.

CHAPTER EIGHT

KATHERINE

The Christmas Party Committee didn't exist before I joined the company. I founded it, so I'm in charge. It consists of me and two other ladies without a personal life. Nevertheless, I take all of my duties very seriously, so I'm the one who has to deal with the band canceling at the last minute.

"I heard Jeff from Legal deejays in his spare time. We can ask him," Maggie offers.

I ponder this for a second. "I want everyone to be able to relax. The whole point of the Christmas party is for everyone to interact freely, lose their inhibitions, and let their hair down. I don't want someone to feel as though they have to step in."

"*You* won't be relaxing," Maggie replies. It's just her and me at this emergency lunch-time meeting three days before the event. "And he'll probably enjoy it."

"We'd need to find equipment and change too many other things." I know I'm just being difficult, but we've always had a band at the Christmas party and I don't want to break tradition. A deejay—especially someone from the firm —doesn't feel special enough. We might as well just put on a Christmas tunes CD and be done with it.

"Where are we going to find a new band this close to the date?" Maggie isn't as passionate about this as I am, which is fine.

"I'll find one." I nod at her resolutely. "Have you ever known me to make a promise and not deliver?" At work, I'm like this. I know I try too much to be one of the guys sometimes, but it's what I do. No man who started at Powell & Cooper with me will become partner before I do.

"No." Maggie shakes her head, then starts getting up. "I need to get back to it. I have full faith in you." She smiles sheepishly. I know what the other women in the company think of me. I don't care.

Once she has closed my office door behind her, I sigh deeply. Solving problems is my job. I usually work them out by arranging numbers so that they add up, but this kind of problem-solving does require a different approach. A challenge. I rack my brain. Then it comes to me. Would Ali West play Christmas songs? I don't have a problem picturing her singing "Winter Wonderland", all the men drooling while they listen—and watch. Or does she only play bars and not perform corporate gigs? There's only one way to find out— and desperate times do call for desperate measures. I reach for the big folder in which I keep all the business cards I've ever received. I flick to the *W* page and there it is.

What will she think when I call her up? It's been weeks since Grace and I ran into her at Temptation, but I distinctly remember her flirting with me at the end of the night. I was so relieved when Grace came back from the bathroom. There's no way in hell I would ever go out with a girl like Ali West. With her reputation and the life she lives?

But that is of no importance now. I need a singer for the party. This will be a business transaction. We will pay her well.

My finger trembles a little when I dial her number. I take a deep breath and go into business mode.

"Hello?" The voice on the other end of the line sounds croaky.

"Hi, Alison. It's Katherine. Katherine Shepherd. You

gave me your card at Temptation a few weeks back. I was wonder—"

"Katherine. Yes. Could you excuse me for just a sec? I'll be right back." I hear the receiver being plonked down carelessly, and muffled voices coming from the other end of the line. Is that a loud yawn? I glance at my watch. It's one p.m. Surely she wasn't still in bed? "Sorry about that. I'm all ears now."

"Do you by any chance play at corporate Christmas parties? I'm looking for someone for this Friday."

"*This* Friday?" Her voice is incredulous.

"Whatever you normally charge, we'll pay you double." I'll pay the difference from my own pocket if I have to.

"You will, huh?" Her tone sounds more serious now. "Which company are you with?"

"Powell & Cooper," I reply.

"So money is no object then. I like that." She pauses. "Let me just quickly double-check my diary, but you may just be giving me a very good excuse to get out of a family dinner I don't really want to attend."

I wait while I hear a groan, the padding of feet and pages being leafed through. "Okay," she says, after a few silent seconds. "I can do it. Here's what I'm going to need."

She sums up the technical equipment while I take meticulous notes.

"It'll just be me and a backing track. I find that it works better than acoustic guitar for occasions like that," she says after specifying the, very short list of equipment she requires. "I do have a Christmas-inspired set list, but you can email me requests if you have any. Please do so as quickly as possible." She sounds surprisingly professional.

"I will." We make further arrangements, agree on a fee and a time to meet, and fifteen minutes after not knowing what to do, I have solved this particular problem, Katherine Shepherd-style.

"Thank you for thinking of me," Alison says. "I

appreciate it."

"I look forward to hearing you sing again." I wouldn't have asked her for this gig if I didn't consider her very good at what she does.

ALI

Over the course of my career, I've played my fair share of Christmas parties. I avoided them at first, until I found out they bring in a lot more dough than a bar gig. They last a bit longer than a regular set, but everyone is usually in very good spirits because of the upcoming holidays, and still well-behaved enough—despite the eggnog—not to embarrass themselves in front of the boss too much.

Sometimes, it's a challenge to get people's attention, because they're not there for the entertainment per se, but I have my way with an audience and if I can convert only three people in a reluctant crowd, I consider the night a success—though I usually convert way more.

When I arrived, Katherine was very business-like. It seemed an odd choice to have her in charge of the entertainment—she doesn't strike me as a very fun-loving person—but when we entered the big meeting room transformed into a ballroom and she started ordering the caterers around, I understood. She gets things done.

I'm only going on in about half an hour, after the big boss has made his speech—Katherine provided me with a minute-by-minute run-down sheet via email yesterday. Earlier, she acted a bit offended when I confessed I hadn't printed it out. But of course she had copies at the ready. She didn't send me any song requests, but I know what to play for an audience like this.

I had wrongly assumed we would have been able to have a chat beforehand, but she's running around from here to there, shaking hands and fake-smiling. By the looks of it, she's not enjoying this party at all—she's working it. So I make it my very specific goal for the night to make Shepherd relax.

As I down a glass of the excellent champagne they serve—big corporations like to go all out for the annual Christmas party—I let my eyes wander over the people I'm about to sing to. Every single one of them is dressed in a suit, even the women. Working for a company like this would mean having to descend into hell every single day for me—though any of my siblings would certainly thrive here. Nessa would make VP in ten years.

"Hey." A woman has come up to me. "I know you."

Irrationally, upon hearing that line, my heart always skips a beat out of fear I'm about to be re-introduced to someone I failed to call back, until it dawns on me that I play all over this city and people might recognize me from a previous gig.

"Do you now?" She's dressed in a skirt suit and, I must admit, it looks damn fine on her.

"I saw you play at Babes-r-Us in L.A. when I was there a few months ago. You had the ladies eating out of the palm of your hand."

"Oh yeah, that was a great gig." It's safe to say I had not expected an encounter like this to happen at this particular event.

"For you, maybe. I saw you leave the party with a very pert blonde and I was none too pleased about that." The woman extends her hand. "Hi, I'm Mia. A fan."

"Nice to meet you, Mia." I take her hand in mine and shake it slowly. "Ali West." I vividly remember the L.A. blonde in question. Not a disappointment at all.

"I had no idea you were playing at Powell & Cooper's esteemed Christmas party. Katherine usually has the same old boring band lined up. This is a very nice surprise."

"I think it's a last-minute thing. I hear the boring dudes

had to cancel due to some emergency."

"Well, hallelujah for that. It's so great to see you again. Makes me feel like I have a second chance, you know?" Mia holds my gaze with a pair of almost-black eyes. She means business. Maybe I'll have to play for her tonight instead of Katherine. None of my vital body parts currently feel as though they want to say no to Mia's obvious advances. I can have an early Christmas present, too.

"Ladies and gentlemen, if I may have your attention, please." An older man has taken to the small stage. "Time to bore you with my annual speech. Good thing Christmas only comes once a year." The crowd breaks out into an obligatory chuckle.

"I'll see you later, Ali. Don't you dare leave this party before saying goodbye to me." Mia grabs my hand and gives it a slight squeeze.

"I wouldn't dare." I watch her dissolve into the crowd and, from the other side of the room, feel Katherine's eyes burn on me. Flirting with her colleagues is probably not in the job description she has for me. But I plead innocent on this one.

★ ★ ★

The gig went well, but I did fail miserably at making Shepherd visibly enjoy my tunes and relax her demeanor. Mia, on the other hand, seemed to appreciate them greatly. After the last encore, and the crowd starts to lose interest, I'm packing up my stuff at the side of the stage when Katherine comes up to me.

"That was great, Ali, but, er…" She stands there shuffling her weight around.

Have there been complaints? I'm all ears. "Yes?"

"I would really appreciate it if you didn't, uh, fraternize with any of the employees. It would reflect badly on me." Of course, she doesn't have the gall to look me in the eyes.

"The gig is over, right?" She paid me upfront, so the money's in the bag as well. "Everyone seemed happy enough with my performance and I think I can safely assume I'm on my private time from now on?" If it weren't Katherine saying this to me, I would be a total professional about this. But our history together—her being uptight and judgmental —makes me want to goad her just for fun. "So, I guess, that what I do as of now is no longer any of your business." I bend myself in her direction a little. "And don't worry, I'll be discreet. No one will ever know. Your reputation is of the utmost importance to me, Katherine."

"I don't want to instruct you on what to do. I know that's not my place." She's gone beet-red. "It just would be unseemly if you were found canoodling with someone from the company."

"Canoodling?" I can't help but chuckle. "You've made your point. The hired help won't embarrass you." I can't believe I tried to hit on her that night at Temptation. Right now, I want to run as far away from her as possible. Grown up or not, Katherine Shepherd and I will never see eye to eye.

"Thanks," she says quickly and walks away.

When I let my gaze flit around the room, I see Mia a few feet away, leaning against the wall. An extra button of her blouse has come undone. She did say I wasn't allowed to leave without saying goodbye. I have no intention of doing so. I wonder which one of the two is higher up in the hierarchy? Perhaps they don't even know about their shared sexual preference.

I swagger over to Mia. "I'm saying goodbye."

"Leaving already?" She cocks her head.

"I've sort of been instructed to." I take a tiny step closer.

"Then I think I'm leaving too." She paints a crooked grin on her face and I can only nod approvingly.

CHAPTER NINE

KATHERINE

Grace and Sandra have gone on a reconciliatory trip to Miami and, per Grace's request, I've gone to Brooklyn to water their plants and have a staycation in their flat.

"There's nothing going on in Midtown," she said. "You're too set in your ways there. You just go from work to home and back, always stopping at the same restaurants and the same grocery store. Do something different just for one weekend. Hell, I'm letting Sandra take me to South Beach after what she did to me."

Grace's suspicions turned out to be correct—I will never doubt her female intuition again—and Sandra had, in fact, struck up an affair with a fellow nurse. She vowed it was all over by the time Grace called her out on it, upon which Grace decided to give her a second chance. At least, she's trying. "No guarantees at all," were her exact words when I spoke to her last.

Out of sorts, I'm wandering along 7th Avenue, unsure what to do with myself. I pass by Temptation, which is closed this time of the afternoon, and briefly consider paying another visit, but I'm not one to go to a bar by myself. Though, perhaps by tonight, I might feel desperate enough. Thinking of Temptation also makes my thoughts drift back to Alison. A few days after the Christmas party—the day before Christmas to be exact—Mia Spaulding came to see me.

"Thank you so much for asking Ali to the Christmas party. She's amazing." She just winked at me and went back on her way. I never even knew she was a lesbian before the party. I wonder if she knows about me—Ali has probably told her by now. I also wonder if she just came by my office to gloat on Ali's insistence because I told her off that night. In hindsight, I shouldn't have done that. My father taught me long ago that you can't tell grown-ups what to do. More often than not, if you do, they'll end up doing the exact opposite of what you asked them. He was right about that.

Now, it's mid-January. Another New Year's celebration has come and gone, and my next birthday is looming. I'll be twenty-seven next month, and more and more, I'm beginning to feel this itch I can't scratch. Not with work, anyway. I don't mind the hours, and I love my job, but, as Grace keeps saying, "There is so much more to life than work."

I used to shrug her off, but now, on the cusp of my next birthday, I'm beginning to think she's right. I want something more for myself. The money keeps piling up in my bank account and I do absolutely nothing with it. I don't have time to spend it. All I've splurged on is a personal trainer whom I meet in the fitness centre across from the office three times a week, and a cleaning lady whom I've taught how to prepare my favorite healthy meals. After which I soon discovered that cooking a meal after work was one of the activities that subconsciously relaxed me the most. I should go on a vacation some time, I think, as I spot a coffee house that looks inviting. I cross the street and head inside.

Once I've ordered a tall latte, I settle down in one of the comfy sofas and grab a book out of my purse. Ironically, it's about a college student falling for one of her female teachers—only an assistant, not a full professor, but still. I found it on Grace and Sandra's coffee table and I can only assume they left it there for me to find.

The tale is strangely compelling, beautifully written, and I can't stop reading—despite the subject matter.

"I love that book," someone says. "Read it cover to cover twice in a row."

I glance up and look into the eyes of a woman.

"I'm sorry. I didn't mean to disturb you, but I saw what you were reading and I couldn't keep my big trap shut." She smiles broadly. "Hi, I'm Susan." She holds out her hand. "I think you have excellent taste in literature and coffee houses. Do you live around here?"

Awkwardly, I shake her hand. "I'm Katherine and I'm staying at a friend's. I live in Manhattan."

"Your loss," Susan says with an even bigger smile on her face. She has a huge mane of blond-ginger curls, held together in the back. "Park Slope is where it's at these days." She briefly purses her lips together. "Can I buy you another cup of coffee, Katherine?"

I don't usually have more than one latte per day, but I'm trying to remember Grace's words. "Live a little," she said. And I could do with the extra caffeine boost in order to converse better with this kind stranger.

"That's very nice of you. I'll have another soy latte, no sugar."

"Coming right up." She winks with one eye and then the other, which is a bit disconcerting.

I watch her scoot off to the counter, and while I do, I will myself to relax. I'm not the best at meeting people, but perhaps Grace was right—again. I can be more relaxed in different surroundings. And a nice woman is buying me coffee. It doesn't hurt that she's easy on the eyes as well.

★ ★ ★

After coffee, Susan takes me to a brand new juice bar halfway between the coffee house and Grace and Sandra's apartment. I have no idea what to order, so I allow her to surprise me.

"You do have that Manhattan vibe about you," she says, after we've sat down. Between us, two enormous mason jars of green juice distract me. This must be a Brooklyn thing.

"What do you mean by that?" Instead of kale juice, I could do with a glass of Pinot Gris to enhance my flirting skills.

"Okay." She smiles broadly, though a little mischievously. This woman I've just met seems to have the textbook version of a winning smile down to a tee. "But just so we're clear, I'm not judging, just observing the differences between us."

"Sure." I smile back. I like how she's at the same time forward and cautious not to say anything upsetting.

"Take your outfit, for instance. You look like you've just come from work."

I can't help but feel a tiny bit offended. I would never go to work dressed like this. I'm not wearing a suit, just slacks, a silk blouse and a cardigan against the chill in the air. But I can play along. This must, after all, be an open invitation for me to comment on Susan's choice of clothing. "I won't lie, you *can* often find me in the office on a Saturday, but not today. Today I'm sitting across from a woman wearing dungarees in a juice bar in Brooklyn. I'm a little out of my comfort zone."

Ostentatiously, she hooks her thumbs underneath the straps of her dungarees and pulls them up. "Do you like my look, Katherine? I'm ready for fashion bloggers roaming the Brooklyn streets any time," she jokes. Susan has that easy, unselfconscious air about her that I've found myself attracted to in the past, yet she's not too loud or crass and respects the boundaries of an initial acquaintance by being polite, though by no stretch boring. Maybe I should ask her out. Maybe this is my time to take the initiative. Grace would be so proud of me.

"I love it." I suck my bottom lip into my mouth and

hold her gaze for an instant.

"This may sound crazy," she says, her voice a little huskier than before. "But I'd really like to have dinner with you some time. There's so much more in this neighborhood I want to show you. Plus, I wouldn't mind getting to know you a little better." The winning smile is back, and seems to have won me over already. She also beat me to the punch, which doesn't come as a surprise.

"I would like that." It sure would beat a lonely night at Grace's apartment during which I scold myself for not going out on my own and watch uninteresting Saturday night television. "I'm free tonight."

"Tonight it is," she says, then drinks from her juice, leaving her with a frothy green mustache on her upper lip.

ALI

Turns out Mia was a keeper. Her blatant come-on at the Powell & Cooper Christmas party might have been a dead giveaway, but I've often encountered women who are very forward under the influence and shrink back into their much more demure personalities in the clear light of day. Not Mia. She is nothing like I expected her to be. I've been seeing her for almost three months now and, even though things are getting serious between us, it doesn't feel that way.

She's not a stickler for domesticity, nor is she obsessed with her work or does she attach too much importance to the number crunching she does for a living. Come to think of it, she's the very definition of casual, and I happen to have a great fondness for casual. Moreover, she seems to really get off on the fact that I'm a singer-songwriter, and never asks me when I'm 'going to start taking my life seriously'.

I'm meeting her at a restaurant near her office. I always

stick out like a sore thumb in places like that, among the suited-up crowds with long-stemmed wine glasses in their hands. I think Mia gets off on that as well. At flaunting me to her co-workers who, inadvertently, always raise an eyebrow when they see us together. I don't mind.

I'm early and scan the crowd. A few suits at the bar. No one I would recognize. While I wait, I consider taking Mia home to meet my family, but they would get too excited about her. It would set expectations I'm nowhere ready to meet. They'd love her, though. I can hear Clayton's annoyingly chirpy voice in my head already. "Way to go, Sis. You're moving up in the world." It would drive me nuts, because, once again, they would be placing value on something that's not important to me. I don't care how much money someone makes, or how many colleagues they oversee at work. I only care about how kind they are, and how they react when I write them a song and, admittedly, also a little about how inventive they are in bed. Mia excels at all those things.

The door of the restaurant opens and Mia walks in. I always feel something flutter inside of me when she enters a room, which, I guess, makes me in love with her. It's a pleasant sensation. She's followed inside by three other people. Colleagues frequenting the same haunts, I presume. Then I see one of them is Shepherd. I do hope Mia hasn't invited Miss Uptight to join us for dinner. Technically, she's the reason Mia and I met—or Mia got her second chance—but if Katherine had gotten her way, and I had abided by her silly rule, we wouldn't be together now. Though, I must admit, the prospect of riling up Shepherd a little, does fill me with glee.

But Shepherd just gives me a quick wave, then heads to the bar where she kisses two women on the cheek and starts chatting.

"Sorry I'm late. I ran into Katherine and you know what a chatterbox she is," Mia jokes.

"Don't I." I waggle my eyebrows. "Busy day at the office, honey?" I give her a warm smile.

"Usual." After Mia has ordered a drink, she asks, "What was Katherine like in college?"

We've never discussed the topic in depth. Mainly because we've been too busy getting to know each other. "The same as now, but worse." I chuckle and glance at Shepherd from the corner of my eye.

"The way she's rising through the ranks at Powell & Cooper, she'd have to be. She's up for yet another promotion. If she keeps this up, she'll be VP before she's thirty."

"I'm sure she would love that." I've still got one eye on Shepherd and I could swear she's stealing furtive glances at me. I bet my presence here makes her uncomfortable. I'm not even sure she has a comfortable mode. If she has, I've never encountered it.

"Some people are just made entirely out of ambition, though rumor has it she's mellowing. Apparently she's seeing someone and she doesn't stay late *every* night anymore." Mia looks at her watch. "It's barely seven and she's already out of the office, though I can tell you with absolute certainty she's talking about work right now."

"Why the fascination with Shepherd?" I ask.

Mia scrunches her lips together and shakes her head. "I'm just curious. She's kind of a legend at work and I know you two have history."

"I wouldn't call it history as such." A giggle rises from deep within me. "Do you want to hear about how we met?"

Mia nods and leans in a little closer. "Do tell."

I tell her about Julianne and how Shepherd walked in on us. I leave out the blackmail part. I wouldn't want Shepherd's colleagues to think any less of her because of that one transgression in college.

"That is hilarious," Mia says. "Of all the people to catch you at it red-handed. That's a tough break."

"Tell me about it. She has looked down on me ever since. As if I'm a lesser creature than her just for being in tune with my more basic urges. If anything, it makes me a better human being, in my humble opinion."

"I wholeheartedly agree, babe," Mia says, and accompanies her statement with a stare I've come to know well, and love.

★ ★ ★

Half an hour later, as I exit a bathroom stall, Shepherd is drying her hands. She clocks me in the mirror.

"You and Mia, huh?" she says. "Who would have thought?"

"Apologies for going against your direct instructions, but, in my defense, she came on to me." I start washing my hands, watching her in the mirror.

"I just didn't want you to—" she starts to say, then gets flustered.

"Start necking on the dance floor." I complete her sentence.

"Well, er, yeah."

She's still standing in front of the hand dryer, so I walk in her direction. "May I?" I wave my wet hands at her. The noise of the dryer makes any conversation impossible for a few seconds, and I can't help but enjoy this moment a little. For as long as I can remember, I've always felt this way around her. Though it might very well be her intention to make me feel bad about myself for the choices I've made, she has only ever achieved the exact opposite.

"I should thank you, really," I say when my hands are dry. "If it weren't for you, Mia and I wouldn't be together." I give her a slow, solemn bow. "So, thank you, Shepherd. You've now officially made up for having Professor Seabolt dump me. The universe is in balance again."

She opens her mouth to say something then, apparently, thinks better of it.

"I hear you're seeing someone." She's starting to get

flustered again. God, she's so easy. "Maybe we should go on a double date some time." With that, I shoot her a quick wink and exit the bathroom, wondering why teasing Katherine Shepherd is such a source of pleasure for me.

CHAPTER TEN

KATHERINE

"Then Katie here broke my heart and told me we weren't right for each other," Grace says.

"She was right," Sandra says.

"How typically lesbian of you to still be best friends," Susan adds. "I've heard the same story a dozen times before."

Susan and I have been seeing each other for six months now, and I spend most of my weekends in Brooklyn these days, despite my heavier workload since I got promoted to manager. When my boss Randy called me into his office and offered me the new job, I jumped at the opportunity—my chest swelling with pride a little when he said I was really the only viable candidate for the position because of my work ethic. If I had known then what I know now, I'm not so sure I would have taken it. Whereas before I could actually finish a to-do list regularly, now new tasks keep adding up and the list has become never-ending. And I have a girlfriend who isn't fond of me working twelve hours a day, every day.

"I always knew I wanted to remain friends with Grace, though it took me a year to convince her to give me another chance." I join the conversation again after having zoned out for a few seconds.

"How persistent of you," Sandra says.

I tilt my head to the side. "She was worth it."

"Oh, I know." Sandra looks at Grace lovingly, as if they're the most perfect couple in the world and she didn't cheat on her last year. Grace is much more forgiving than I am. I still can't look at Sandra and think of what she did, though they seem to be doing okay. According to Grace, Sandra is a different person now, and she's glad they didn't break up in the end. True love conquers all and all that. When I told Susan about what happened, I made it very clear that I would never in my life display that amount of tolerance towards infidelity.

"Don't I know it," Susan said. "I have all the Katherine Shepherd rules memorized and stored in my head. Don't you worry."

"It's not because we're still friends now that you breaking up with me didn't hurt me terribly at the time." Grace is not letting it go.

"We were so young back then," I reply. "What was I supposed to have done?"

Grace shoots me a wide smile, then addresses Susan. "She falls for it every time."

Susan pulls me close to her and kisses me on the cheek. "But we love her for it."

Heat travels under my skin. Not just because of Susan's touch, but because of how being with her makes me feel. There's definitely room for improvement in my life—I assume there always will be—but I can't remember a time when I was happier. I have a job I love, with a company that appreciates me, and I have a serious girlfriend who adores me and whom I adore right back. This is not far off from the life I dreamed up for myself when I was a teenager and first realized I was attracted to girls.

I give Susan a peck on the cheek back, then become suddenly aware of how tired I am. It's Saturday, but I was in the office at six this morning in order to make it to Susan's place for lunch. I stifle a yawn.

"Someone needs her bed," Susan says.

We say our goodbyes to Grace and Sandra, who invited us to dinner, then walk the few minutes to Susan's building.

"So," Susan says as she grabs my hand. "You seem to have taken a shine to Brooklyn."

"I love it. And I love you." I lean into her a little.

"Why don't you move here then?" She stops walking. "Move in with me."

It's true that I spend more of my free time here than I do at my own apartment, but I hadn't seen this coming at all. Isn't it too soon? And what about my commute?

"Felix is not going to like that," I say, stupidly. "Poppy doesn't seem like a very easy-going cat and I can't imagine Felix enjoying her company."

"Never mind how the cats may feel about it, babe. What do *you* think?" She smiles her smile. The one I can't possibly say no to. I've never lived with anyone before, though it's always a little hard to say goodbye to Susan on Sunday evenings. During the week, when I usually sleep alone in my own bed, I've come to miss her warm body against mine.

"I think I wouldn't mind giving it a try." I kiss her on the forehead.

"We'll tell Poppy and Felix together," Susan says, and puts her head on my shoulder as she pulls me close.

ALI

I hadn't seen Anna in more than a year, when all of a sudden she turned up at my front door with a suitcase in her hand.

"I've left her," she said. "I was so sick of being someone's wife."

After I yelled at Mia to put on some clothes, I invited her in and gave her a long hug. Anna Davis. My estranged friend. But no matter how estranged we might have gotten, with some people you can just pick right up where you left things last. Anna is one of those people. She has been my sister-in-arms for so long. The bond we forged in college will never be broken. I will always be there for her, just as she will for me. We don't need to check in with each other every week to know that. We don't even need to see each other regularly to feel that connection.

She hasn't met Mia yet, and is very apologetic about barging in on us like that on a Sunday morning. Mia is the kind of person who understands this sort of stuff without needing it explained to her, and makes herself scarce for the rest of the afternoon.

"Hot damn," Anna says, after Mia has left. "Ali West shacked up with a hot chick. Who would have thought?"

"We're hardly shacked up," I reply, though we're not exactly not-shacked-up either. Mia loves my place, so we end up staying here most of the time, but it's not as if she has officially moved in.

"Tell me what happened with Grayson," I ask, while I pour us some coffee.

"Nothing happened. I just woke up this morning and I knew I had to get out. When I tried to conjure up images of us ten, twenty years down the road, I could never picture myself with a smile on my face. She started talking about children the other day, and I just… couldn't. Not that I don't want children, I just… I don't know, Ali. Maybe it's cruel to say this about a woman I've been madly in love with the last few years, but I knew for a fact I didn't want children with her."

"You fell out of love. It happens all the time." I give her a thorough once-over. She's still the Anna who would tell me off in college. Her hair is still dyed ginger and she still has that semi-condescending glare in her eyes.

"Maybe long-term relationships are just not for me. I felt so stifled. So dependent on someone else for my happiness. It's not how I want my life to be. Then I thought of you. How you live your life. So free of… everything. Though, I must admit, while I had expected to find a girl in your bed on a Sunday morning, I hadn't expected her to be your girlfriend."

"Mia's cool. She doesn't have wild expectations, nor does she want me to commit or anything like that. We're monogamous, yet casual, if that's even a thing."

"I guess it is now." Anna eyes me intently. "God, is it good to see you. I've missed you, Ali."

"You can stay here as long as you like."

Anna looks around. "As much as I would like to be your roommate, this loft isn't exactly suited for it, what with it not having any inner walls to speak of and such." She tilts her head. "Nor would I want to encroach on you and your lady."

"We'll figure it out." I pat Anna's hand.

"That's what I love about you, Ali. You always figure it out." She looks around, until her gaze halts. "Do you play guitar now? When is your next gig? You can be sure I'll be there. God, the hours I've watched you on stage. I was basically your first groupie."

I follow her gaze and glance at my guitar. "My mother has convinced me to help her run a new charity program she just founded. She called it Music For The Children. What I really think is that she started it so I could at least have a semblance of a normal job, instead of just playing gigs all the time, so basically it's more like Music For *Her* Child, but I have to say I'm kind of enjoying it."

Anna shakes her head. "I don't understand why you haven't hit the big time yet. You're so talented. So much better than anyone in the charts." I've missed Anna. She was always my biggest cheerleader.

"I've never been very interested in making it big. I just want to sing, not suck up to music industry douchebags. Believe me, I've been there, and I ran a mile."

"It helps that you're a West, I guess." If anyone else

said that to me, my hackles would go up automatically, but not when Anna does. I know she doesn't mean to insinuate anything.

"And I'm the baby West," I say. "I pretty much get away with anything."

"Did you meet Mia at a gig?" she asks.

"I did, though not the sort I would usually pick someone up at. It was a corporate Christmas party, and you'll never guess who invited me to play." I relish telling Anna the story of how I ended up with Mia. Once I have, she looks at me, shaking her head.

"Life can be funny that way," she says. "If you hadn't had an affair with your French professor in college, you probably wouldn't have met Mia."

"It's all connected." A smile splits my lips. "I wrote a song about how little occurrences like that can alter the course of your life. Do you want to hear it?"

"Of course," Anna shouts.

I grab my guitar and start to play.

PART THREE

2008

CHAPTER ELEVEN

KATHERINE

'Welcome back, Class of 1998' the banner says. If it weren't for Susan insisting that we'd come, I wouldn't be here. I have better things to do with my time than reminisce. But Susan has a love-hate relationship with NYU—she applied but got rejected—and tonight she wants to explore the love side of it.

"A lot of my memories here are with Grace," I say as I glance around nervously, though I don't know why I'm nervous. A while back I received an email from the alumni association that has organized this reunion and was asked to send them back some information on my current occupation and any notable achievements since graduating. Two weeks ago I got the email compiling all the gathered information and while there was one person whose profession was stated as CEO, it's of his own mid-sized company. I'm Assistant Chief Financial Officer at Powell & Cooper at the age of thirty-two so, in terms of professional success, I'm leading the pack. On top of that, I have Susan by my side. We've been together for more than five years. We just bought a brownstone in Brooklyn. Things are going swimmingly.

For the most part, reunions are just an open invitation to show off, so show off I shall—seeing as small talk is not my forte.

"Did Grace come to her ten-year reunion last year? I

don't remember her mentioning it," Susan says.

"She didn't. She couldn't really face it just then." After four more years of trying, Grace finally had enough of Sandra and her cheating. She was sad for a few months, but has since adopted Sandra's philandering ways, though of course she's single, so she's not cheating on anyone while playing the field.

"Katherine Shepherd? Is that you?" A tall ginger man walks up to us. His name tag says Robert and I can still see a resemblance to that guy who often sat next to me in Advanced Economic Theory.

"Robert Haines. I can't believe it." And so it begins, I think, as I shake his outstretched hand. He has a firm grip, but so do I.

I introduce him to Susan and he talks about how he became head accountant of a big law firm. More familiar faces join our group and, before long, despite not being one for nostalgia, I find I'm enjoying this trip down memory lane.

Most of the people I speak to are married with children and, to my surprise—because I believed things had changed—almost fifty percent of the women I graduated with have become stay-at-home moms. Not one of the men has become a stay-at-home dad.

"Well, well, well." I recognize her voice instantly. "If it isn't the Chief Financial Officer at Powell & Cooper."

Alison doesn't appear to have brought a date. She played at our Christmas party two more times, but after she and Mia parted ways, she was banned. Not that I still have time to occupy myself with such mundane tasks as organizing company parties.

I haven't seen Ali West for years. She looks slightly older than when I saw her last, but the passing of time doesn't seem to have a big hold on her. She looks at least ten years younger than anyone else present here. Though she is dressed a bit more maturely and no longer wears a dozen bangles around her wrists and those velvety jackets I used to see her in.

"Assistant CFO," I say.

"But probably not for much longer," Susan says. "She'll be CFO soon enough."

I give Susan a puzzled look. There has never been any talk of that. Bruce, the current CFO, is in perfect health and has not given any signs of wanting to leave the company. Perhaps my ambition burns so bright it has given my significant other a glimpse into my soul. We live together. She knows me well. Still, her comment is inappropriate. I'm glad, however, that she only uttered it in front of Ali West, who, I suspect, doesn't much care for these things. Thank heavens Robert is no longer standing around.

I introduce Susan to Ali.

"We were in French class together," Ali says.

"You speak French?" Susan asks. "I had no idea."

"I should never have taken French." I eye Ali, who looks straight back at me. "I wasn't very good at it."

"Must have been the professor," Ali says. "What was her name again? Sea… something. Do you remember, Katherine?"

"Seabolt," I'm quick to say.

"Ah, yes, that's right. Seabolt. How could I have forgotten?" She stares straight into my eyes with her dark brown ones. It's an unsettling feeling. One that takes me back to that time she almost hit on me in that lesbian bar years ago. Then I realize that she was just playing me. Of course she remembers Professor Seabolt's name.

Some things never change.

"Still taking New York stages by storm?" I ask. "Alison is a singer," I inform Susan.

In the alumni newsletter listing our occupations, it didn't say anything underneath Alison's picture. She's probably not the type to reply to emails in a timely fashion.

"How wonderful," Susan says. "So much more exciting

than all the lawyers and accountants here."

"It has become more of a hobby of late," Alison says, surprising me. "I work for a charity called Music For The Children these days. I teach them all about pop music and guitar chords."

"Wow." Susan seems genuinely in awe of Ali. The only times I've ever been impressed with her were when she took to the stage—where she so clearly belongs.

"I do what I can," Alison says, in that loose-limbed way of hers, her voice low and relaxed.

"Sorry things didn't work out with you and Mia." I'm not a person my colleagues confide in, not even lesbian colleagues who break up with an acquaintance of mine. One day, Mia just sent me an email to say she and Alison had broken up, and that was that. Alison West's name was never mentioned again in the corridors of Powell & Cooper.

"Water under the bridge." Ali shrugs. "That was a long time ago."

ALI

Shepherd has aged well. That overly tense girl who yelled at me outside one of the buildings of this fine establishment more than ten years ago has turned into a pretty gorgeous thirty-something. She still dresses like a middle-aged Catholic school teacher, though.

After I say my goodbyes to her and her partner to greet a bunch of other people—and avoid a few others—my mind keeps drifting to her. After the speeches, I locate her in the crowd and watch her for a bit while I engage in small talk with people from way back when.

Graceful would be the correct way to describe her. If only her drunk friend hadn't interrupted me that night when I played at Temptation. I know Shepherd is probably convinced she could never be lured into bed by the likes of me, but I've seduced many a woman who never thought she'd be swayed to spend time between my sheets.

Ever since things went south between Mia and me, I haven't been involved in anything serious.

"You practice very short bouts of serial monogamy," Anna said not long ago. We now share a two-bedroom apartment not far from where I used to live. After getting used to having someone around, I found myself actually feeling lonely when I came home to my big, empty loft. That loft belongs in my twenties, and I'm almost thirty-two now. Just as singing on stage at least three times a week is something relegated to the previous decade of my life. I still love to sing—I do it all the time—but I don't crave the stage as much as I used to.

Admittedly, if Shepherd had come alone, I might have had another crack at her, just for old times' sake. Even if it hadn't gone anywhere, then just for fun.

Regal would be another word to describe her. A quality that never interested me much before, but my taste in women seems to evolve with age as well. I let my gaze drift from Shepherd, and scan the various groups gathered around high tables. In one of them, I see at least two women I slept with. They're both here with their husbands now.

"Hey stranger." Jennifer walks up to me, her wife in tow. She throws her arms around me and gives me a big hug. "Where's your other bestie at?"

"Anna? She wouldn't be caught dead at one of these."

"And you would?" Jen asks.

"Just representing the Wests of Park Avenue. You know me, I take my family obligations very seriously."

Jen and I both snicker, while her wife Cindy looks on.

"Shepherd is here." I nod in Katherine's direction.

Jen looks confused. She has no reason to remember. "Oh, didn't you and her once, you know?"

I shake my head vigorously. "No. Nothing like that,"

I'm quick to say. "She got me a gig once." It's interesting how, over the course of the years, Shepherd has gone from the girl who caught me canoodling with our professor to the woman who got me a gig. Maybe my perception of her has changed over the years as well.

"Are you interested?" Jen asks, a crooked grin on her face.

"Nah."

"How long have I known you? I can tell that you are," Jen says.

I'm not one to lie to myself or anyone else about these things. "Maybe under different circumstances." I glance at Shepherd again. She has her hand on her partner's shoulder.

"There's plenty more fish in the sea, buddy," Jen says.

I look around the room. I don't spot many single fish.

★ ★ ★

An hour later, I've consumed too much wine and have not eaten enough of the canapés that are going around. I've made my appearance. I'm no longer interested in hearing about my former classmates' uneventful lives. Exactly no one here has surprised me with a twist in their life story. And I've heard way too much chatter about children I will never meet.

I tap Jen on the shoulder. "I think I'm gonna go."

"Already?" She gives me a once-over. "Is the cheap booze having a nasty effect on you?"

"You could say that."

Jen throws her arms around me and so does Cindy, then I take my leave. I nod at a few people as I move towards the exit, and get stopped a couple of times for a brief, meaningless chat. When I try to catch one last glimpse of Shepherd before she disappears from my life again until the next reunion, or the next time life puts us together in a room, I can't find her.

Ah well, I think, some things are never meant to be. I also know that the reason why I have this flicker of interest in her is because I can't have her, and because of the challenge she represents. I barely know her, and what I do know of her I don't even particularly like. She's hot, though. I shake my head, chastizing myself for even thinking like that. I'm at my ten-year college reunion, but if you were to take a look at the inside of my mind, you'd think I was still in high school.

"Leaving so soon?" Shepherd is leaning against the outside wall of the West library.

"What are you doing at the library? Still not studied enough?" Something pulses in my stomach. It might be the booze.

"I was giving Susan a tour. She's just gone to wash her hands." Shepherd has pushed herself away from the wall and shuffles her weight around.

A flashback makes its way to the forefront of my mind. Me and Shepherd near that bench over there, shouting at each other. "Remember when you yelled at me over there." I point at the bench.

"I yelled at you?" She crosses her arms in front of her chest. "I'm sure that if I did, you only had yourself and your callous ways to blame for that."

"For some reason, you always ended up yelling at me when our paths crossed. I'm glad things have changed over time." I sway on my feet a little, giving her one of my well-practiced looks—though I know I shouldn't.

"Not always," she says, her voice firm.

"Do you think there's a reason why we keep meeting like this?" I throw in a crooked smile.

"What do you mean? We're at our college reunion. Of course we were going to see each other."

I wasn't really expecting her to meet me halfway in this extremely mild flirtation, and at least I have learned something. Katherine Shepherd doesn't have a playful bone in her body. Everything is serious with her. She would be too much of a challenge.

"You're right. Silly me." I give her a quick nod. "I'd best be on my way then. Enjoy the rest of your evening." With that, I walk away from her, probably for the last time.

CHAPTER TWELVE

KATHERINE

"Was that the singer?" Susan has come back from the bathroom. "She's the most fascinating person I've met here tonight."

"Oh really?" I'm still wondering what Ali was getting at. And, I might be mistaken, but she was giving off a flirty vibe. How utterly disrespectful of her.

"Well, yeah." Susan shakes her head. "I hate to be the one to tell you, but the NYU Class of 1998 has not done many thrilling things with their lives. Except for you, of course, babe. You went for a walk in Brooklyn one day and met this catch of a woman." She slides an arm around my waist. "You really don't remember any French?" she whispers in my ear.

"*Bonsoir, Madame,*" I whisper back. "*Comment allez-vous?*" Just saying a few words in French takes me right back to being in Professor Seabolt's class and how inadequate that made me feel. To that image of her lips smudged with lipstick. And to that wretched, guilty sensation in the pit of my stomach when I received my final grade. I've never even told Susan about it. It's not exactly information you share with someone you're dating, and then, afterwards, it just never came up.

We walk back to where the party is. "She's someone I'd like to get to know better. She could be an interesting friend to have," Susan says.

"Who? Alison?" Why is she still going on about her? "She's not friend material."

"Why not?" Susan insists. "Did something happen between the two of you?"

"God no, not like that anyway. My only girlfriend in college was Grace."

Susan bumps her hip into mine. "Why don't you like her? You acted so skittishly around her."

"Skittish?" I stop just before we're about to re-enter the main building. "Because of her I did something in college I'm not proud of. I'd really just rather forget about her."

Susan quirks up her eyebrows. "Now you've got me curious. You? Katherine Shepherd? Did you break the rules? How thrilling!"

"It's not something I feel very comfortable discussing out here, but I'll tell you later, I promise." I'm actually enjoying the look on Susan's face. "But don't get your hopes up, it's nothing too spectacular."

★ ★ ★

"You blackmailed your professor?" We're in a taxi back to Brooklyn. "You?"

"It was more than ten years ago, Suze. No need to make a big deal about it." I am getting a little worked up, though. "Besides, I would never have done it if it weren't for her... behaving the way she did. She was taking advantage of a student."

"Hm. Alison doesn't strike me as the kind of girl who would let someone take advantage of her." Susan breaks out into a smile. "I bet she instigated it. Went up to the professor and started flirting with her. You can hardly blame the woman for not resisting her." Susan pulls her phone out of her pocket. "What was the professor's name again?"

"Why? What are you doing?"

"Googling her, of course. I want to know what she looks like. They should really invite professors to reunions. I would love to have seen *that* particular reunion."

"Why are you getting so worked up about this?"

Susan pats my knee. "I'm just having a little fun, babe. My partner has just told me she blackmailed her professor in college. Is it any wonder I want to dig a little deeper?"

"You think Ali's hot, don't you?" I glare at Susan. "That's why you're getting so excited."

"I'm not blind, babe," she says, deadpan. "There's not a living creature on this earth who wouldn't think Ali's hot. She's smoking. Those eyes. Christ, it felt as though she was looking straight into my soul with them. And that luxurious smile." Susan fans herself. "I need to know what that professor looked like. Come on, us lesbians have to make our own entertainment, you know that."

"Is that why you want to become friends with her? Because she's hot?" Frankly, I'm starting to feel a bit jealous, but I can't let Susan get as much as an inkling of that. She'll tease me mercilessly if she does.

"Why not?" I think the teasing might have started already. "She's hot and interesting. Why would we not want to hang out with her? Surely what she did in college was much worse than you making the most of a bad situation. Are you afraid she's going to use it against you?" She taps on her phone a few times. "Ah, I've found her. Oh my." She stares at her phone. "I can totally see it."

I exhale a deep sigh. I gaze out of the window, but we're still a while away from home, so it looks like I'll have to endure this pointless chatter a while longer.

"She's no longer teaching at NYU, it says here," Susan says. "Must have slept with one student too many." Susan turns to me. "Did you never have a crush on any of your teachers, babe? Can you imagine acting on that and actually having it work? That Ali is one badass chick."

"You might be feeling under her magic spell at the moment, but I simply don't like her very much. I never have. I don't like what she stands for and I certainly don't like the way she had the nerve to speak to me when we were in college. We're totally different people and we could never be friends."

"All right. All right." Susan holds up her hands. "I was just having a little fun." She puts her head on my shoulder. "You're a badass too, babe." She gives a chuckle.

I've never in my life used the word badass, let alone felt like one.

ALI

"How was the big reunion?" Anna asks over a late breakfast on Sunday morning. Despite arriving home before midnight, I woke up with a splitting headache. Anna has brought me a cup of strong coffee, a glass of freshly-pressed orange juice and a plate of scrambled eggs in bed, and now huddles with me under the covers.

"As you expect these things to go. You didn't miss anything. Jen says hi."

"That woman," Anna says. "She has become the complete opposite of what I had expected her to become. It's like our personalities were switched."

I shake my head. "Nonsense. You're still as judgmental as you were in college." I'm glad my sense of humor is making its way from underneath the dark veil of my hangover.

"Hey." Anna elbows me in the ribs. "I'm as much a changed woman as you are."

"Have I changed?" I suddenly really want to know how she sees my evolution over the years.

"Oh, yes. Time has taken its toll on Ali West as well," Anna jokes. "No more weekend benders for you. No more after-midnight gigs."

"Seriously, Anna. How am I different than in college?

And I don't mean physically."

"You're more mature. You no longer sleep with a different woman every weekend. You have a respectable roommate. You even have a proper job. Who would have thought?"

"I'm nothing like anyone I saw again last night, I can tell you that. They all seemed to take everything so seriously. Their career. Starting a family. I was talking to Peggy Byrne, do you remember her? She wasted no time in telling me she's had five fertility treatments. What was I supposed to say to that?"

"That's exactly the reason I didn't go. I can't stand having conversations like that with people I barely even knew ten years ago. It's torture."

"Though, I have to say that… I don't know how to explain it." I sit up a bit straighter to collect my thoughts. "Most of these people did have a well-defined purpose in life. I can't say I ever really had that. I used to be convinced I didn't need it. Now, I'm not so sure anymore."

"But you do have a purpose, Ali. You work with children. You teach them about the deep, mysterious beauty of music. Sharing that with them is one damn fine purpose to have in life, to make them aware of that so young in life, lest they all grow up thinking that Taylor Swift and Flo-Rida are all there is to music."

"The other day I was playing them some Indigo Girls. They loved it. I taught them how to sing along to the chorus of "Closer to Fine". One of the better moments of my career." I fondly remember a group of fifteen children between the ages of six and eleven singing along with me. "But I wasn't talking about work. I'll be thirty-two soon and I've had one serious relationship. That's it. What does that say about me?"

"Gosh, you are gloomy this morning, Ali. I'm so glad I didn't go to that reunion. I will, however, employ my chirpy spirit to cheer you up." She tucks her legs under her behind and fastens her gaze on me. "I had a very serious relationship, and what does that say about me?" She pulls up her shoulders. "Absolutely nothing, because it could mean so many different things. Maybe I just haven't met the right woman yet; or maybe Grayson was one of the few right women that destiny has intended me to be with over the course of my life. I don't know. What I do know, however, is that I don't need to be in a relationship to be happy. I'm not saying it can't get lonely at times, but that's what friends are for. I'm telling you, Ali, moving in with you has been really good for me. I can only hope I have the same effect on you."

I can't help but smile when Anna says something like that. I already know she will make someone—or multiple ones—very happy some day. Which brings another thought to my head. "Maybe we should make one of those pacts you see in movies. If we're both still single by the time we're forty, we should just marry each other."

Anna nods approvingly. "I could marry into some of that West money. Sure." She holds out her hand. "Let's shake on it."

I play along and shake her hand. As our palms meet, Anna starts pulling me out of bed. "Let's not waste our Sunday. Let's go meet some women, Ali. When I go out with you, they seem to flock to me like bees to honey. That's what you are: my honeypot." She giggles uncontrollably.

When she's done, I say, "Katherine Shepherd was there."

"Were you expecting Mademoiselle Perfect not to be there?" Anna asks.

"No, I just… It was strange seeing her again."

"Why? Because of Mia?"

"No." I shrug. "I don't know. She's different now, but also still the same. She seems to have this effect on me. An effect I don't like. I can't really put my finger on it. But she sure has turned into a fine specimen of a woman."

"So you have the hots for her?" Anna inquires, a

quizzical look on her face.

I don't know where I'm going with this either. "Maybe a little, but she's impossible. It's like she has no sense of humor at all. But I still kind of like her, I don't know why."

"Did you… try anything?"

"No. She's with someone. I wouldn't do that."

"Well, then… this proves my point. Get your glad rags on, West. We're going to a lesbian tea dance."

"A what?" I groan.

"They're all the rage these days and are basically just an excuse for heavy drinking—and flirting—on a Sunday afternoon." She grabs my hand again. "Come on, my honeypot. Your bee needs you." She makes a buzzing noise with her lips.

I push Shepherd to the back of my mind where she belongs and head to the shower.

PART FOUR

2014

CHAPTER THIRTEEN

KATHERINE

The absolute last thing I want to do tonight is be faced with Grace's new girlfriend, a woman she met in P-town of all places—during Women's Week, of course. But Grace is my best friend, and she's been there for me during this break-up unequivocally, and I know how important me meeting this woman is to her. After all, she could be the new Sandra, minus the cheating. It's the prospect of staring young, abundant love in the face that puts me off the most. Still, I apply my usual amount of understated make-up, slip into my restaurant clothes, and exit my brand new apartment in Midtown—it seemed like the most logical place to move to after Susan and I split up. There was no way I was staying in Brooklyn. To me, Brooklyn equals Susan, and Susan is out of my life now. Thus, so is Brooklyn.

Thank goodness we're meeting at a place in Chelsea tonight, because I certainly don't feel like schlepping all the way across the bridge. I hail a cab and on the drive over, I inspect my face in a hand-held mirror. I wouldn't want Grace's new woman to get the impression I'm falling apart, even though I am.

We're having drinks at a new bar called Medusa first and the cab drops me just in front. It's moodily lit with sparse, but brightly glowing lamps and, as I walk through the door, I think I could easily polish off a bottle of Pinot just as a starter. I take a deep breath and straighten my spine. It's not my style to wallow, but perhaps that's because I've never felt the need before.

Grace waves at me from a table in the back, all happy-faced. I paint on the best smile I can muster and appreciate the heartfelt hug she gives me.

"Katie, please meet Anna and vice-versa."

"Very pleased to meet you." I try to give Anna my hand to shake, but she pulls me into a hug instead. How very forward of her.

"Anna's best friend should be here any minute," Grace says. "Ah, there she is already."

I turn around and look straight into Alison West's face.

Oh Christ. Any night but tonight.

"If it isn't Katherine Shepherd." Ali bows ostentatiously—annoyingly. "Nice to see you again." At least she doesn't hug me, but just shakes my hand.

"Ali."

"Of course!" Anna slaps her hand against her forehead. "They know each other," she says to Grace. "We were all at NYU together"—she pauses to do the math.

"Class of '98," I say, "so sixteen years ago."

All four of us sit down and I end up facing Ali, while I could really do with Grace's friendly face opposite mine right now. First, it's time for the obligatory what-do-you-do round of questions. I'm almost baffled to learn that Ali now heads a charity that introduces inner city kids to music. I guess people can change.

"I'm CFO of Powell & Cooper," I explain to Anna. "Lots of numbers and meetings." Two weeks ago, for the very first time since starting work at P & C fifteen years ago, I had to take a sick day. I woke up in the morning and the prospect of even lifting my leg and slipping it from underneath the covers was enough to cause another bout of crying. Susan and I have been separated for a month and a half now, but it only recently started to hit me, with some sort of sadistic delayed effect. At first, I just focused on work and I was getting so much more done. But now, I find I can't even rely on the comfort of going to work anymore to keep my mind off the break-up.

"Are you still with, er... I'm sorry, I forgot her name?" Alison asks.

An uncomfortable silence descends. Grace could have asked Anna to warn Ali not to ask painful questions.

"Susan," I say, a sob in my voice. "No." Just saying the word *no* feels like the bottom being pulled from underneath my life all over again. Eleven years together and then nothing. Nothing but this pain in my chest and this frost in my heart.

"I'm sorry." Ali does look genuinely apologetic, but it's too late now. My mind went there. What could Susan be doing right now? Does she still think of me, or is it all Phoebe for her now all the time? "I had no idea."

"It's fine." I wave her off and take a large gulp of wine. I'm ordering something stronger after this. Fuck my health. What good does it do me anyway?

"You do know how these two met, right?" Anna asks Grace. "It's the most outrageous story."

There used to be a time when I always at the very least flinched at being reminded of that ordeal, but now it barely registers. I need to pull myself together. I came here to make a good impression on Grace's new girlfriend, whom she is completely besotted with. Moreover, I don't want to fall apart in front of Alison West. It's been a month and a half, six weeks. I should be able to deal with it better by now.

Grace and Anna only have eyes for each other and are giggling over the story of my bursting in on Ali and Seabolt.

Ali shoots me an apologetic look. "I guess that will always have an amusement factor to it."

"I guess." I want to make small talk, I really do, but even under the best of circumstances I'm already so bad at it. I should have trusted my gut and stayed home tonight.

Ali leans over the table. "Are you sure you're all right, Katherine?"

I steel myself. "I will be," I reply. I will be because I want to be. "I—I haven't been out much since…"

"Oh my God," Grace suddenly exclaims. "I remember now." She looks at Ali. "You played at Temptation years ago. Katie and I were both there. We saw you sing. You were amazing. That's about all I remember from that night."

Ali does that head tilt she does. "That's right."

"It's a small world," Anna says. "If only I'd been there that night. Maybe we could have met already." She smiles at Grace sheepishly. These two have got it good.

"That was a different time," Ali says. "Maybe you wouldn't have been ready yet. I believe things happen at the right time for a reason."

If I were feeling like myself at all, I'd certainly be quizzing her about that statement, but I feel like a hollow shell with a mask that looks like my face glued on, so I don't say anything.

"I believe we have a restaurant reservation at eight," Grace says and looks at her watch. "It's just around the corner. Shall we go?"

ALI

Shepherd looks shaken to the core. Her body is physically present, but her mind is clearly elsewhere. From what's been said tonight, I gather the break-up with Susan must have been recent and bad. I can't even needle her about things. I feel sorry for her. Maybe I should rescue her from this situation. She's probably only here to support her best friend and to meet Anna, and there will be plenty more occasions for that.

As we shuffle out of the bar, I tap her on the shoulder,

and say, "Hey, do you want me to get you out of here?"

"What—what do you mean?" I detect some make-up on her face, but it's doing a bad job of hiding the black circles under her eyes.

"Let's bail. I'll take you home. We'll do some—" I swallow the word *blow* just in time. "We'll have a drink."

"Do you really have the audacity to hit on me right now?" she sneers. "How dare you."

"Katherine, no. I'm just trying to help. I see how you're suffering. Frankly, Grace is your best friend and she should see it too, but she's too busy falling in love. Just as we can't hold that against them, they can't hold it against us if we bail right now."

"Us? You don't have to leave because of me. I can take —"

I grab her by the arms, and complete her sentence. "You can take care of yourself. I'm sure you can."

"Hey, you guys," Anna shouts from the corner of the street. "Come on, we're going to be late."

"Do you want to go home? Just nod and I'll make it happen."

Shepherd gives the slightest nod.

"Stay here. Don't move. I'll be right back."

I hurry over to the corner, apologize as much as I can to Grace and Anna, and tell them Katherine is feeling unwell, they should have a good time together, and we'll do this again soon. I don't give them time to reply. Before they can gather their thoughts and inquire about Katherine's well-being, I've turned around and am back by Katherine's side.

"Direct me to your castle," I say, trying a little grin on her.

I look behind me and Anna and Grace are waving at us. They're not stupid. They get what's going on here. Katherine is a heartbroken mess.

"I live in Midtown. I guess we can walk."

"My apartment is really close by, just for your

information. But wherever you want to go is fine." I'm not used to dealing with fragile adults, but I guess just being nice will help the most.

Katherine nods. "My place barely has any furniture. I only moved in a few weeks ago."

"Come on." Ever so gently, I press my palm against the small of her back and coax her in the right direction.

✳ ✳ ✳

"I used to live here with Anna, until her grandmother left her an apartment in the Village. By then, I guess, we'd spent enough time living together," I say while I pour Katherine a stiff measure of bourbon.

She lets her gaze drift over my living room, which isn't exactly spotless, but that's the way I like it. I hate living spaces where everything is just so and that don't look the slightest bit lived-in.

I sit down in the armchair to her left and slip a leg under my knee, making myself comfortable. "Do you want to talk about it?"

When she looks at me her eyes are filled with tears. Knowing what I know about Katherine Shepherd and, granted, I don't know that much, this must be so hard on her. Because I do know that she's not one to wear her heart on her sleeve and here she sits, unable to hide her emotions, battling with a pain so raw it's even visible in the way she sits, her shoulders slumped and her chin tilted down.

"She fell in love with someone else." She takes a quick sip and wraps her fingers around the belly of the glass. "Hence, out of love with me."

"Shit. That's harsh."

"We had a life together. Eleven years is a long time. And now, I feel as though I have nothing left. Not even myself."

"I'm so sorry, Katherine." I figure that if I don't say too much, she'll just keep on talking.

She does.

"The only saving grace is that she didn't cheat on me. Though honestly I don't care, because I don't really see the difference in inflicted pain between the two. In fact, if she'd just slept with someone else it would have hurt me far less than what she's done now. It's just gut-wrenching to hear the woman that you love and you believe you're going to grow old with profess her love for someone else. Honestly, I don't wish it on my worst enemy. It just completely… diminishes you. That's how I feel. Diminished. Insignificant. A mere nuisance to her, really."

"I can see how that would have done a number on you, but, you know, these things happen."

I must have said the wrong thing because she suddenly glares at me. "Have you ever been dumped? Have you ever been put outside with the trash that's stinking up the house? Traded in for a newer model? I'm a cliché now—so is she, by the way. I begged and pleaded for her to see reason, to wait for her infatuation to pass. Which couple hasn't gone through that? But oh no, Susan Williston was following her passion. It's just… hard to see an up-side to all of this."

"When did it happen?" I notice Katherine has emptied her glass already. She doesn't look like a heavy drinker and a few of these will probably knock her out, but maybe that's just what she needs right now. To just forget about it all for a night. Though it will hurt extra in the morning. I hold up the bottle, and she nods.

"A month and a half ago, and you know what the real kicker was?" She holds out her glass for a refill. "I didn't have a clue. I did not see it coming at all. My partner of eleven years had been falling in love with someone else for months and I was completely oblivious to it. What does that say about me?" She drinks again.

"Sometimes we notice least what's happening right under our noses."

A silence falls. I drink as well.

Then she says, "Why are you being so nice to me?"

"Why wouldn't I be nice to you?"

That gives her pause. "Did you know I was Grace's best friend and that you were meeting me tonight?"

"Honestly, no. I've hardly seen Anna in the last couple of months and the name Grace is not that uncommon. I haven't seen you in years so I didn't put two and two together. Though I do find it amusing."

"Amusing, huh?"

"You have to admit it's a little bit funny." I try a smile again.

"I guess it is. Of all the women Grace could have fallen for, she goes and falls for your best friend."

"During Women's Week in P-town," I add. "Anna asked me to go with her, but I politely declined."

"Grace didn't even ask me. She knows I would never go."

I try to stifle a chuckle, but it doesn't work.

"Why are you laughing?" Katherine asks, but she must know, because the tiniest of smiles is breaking on her face.

"I was just trying to picture you in P-town during Women's Week."

"It's just not for me. Too rowdy. Too many women in one place."

I'm glad I got her off the topic of her break-up, though I do wonder how she would know what it would be like in Provincetown if she's never been. Wisely, I decide to give her a break and not quiz her on that, in case it pushes her back into the direction of the previous topic—and into more wallowing in her own misery. "It's pretty cool, actually. I played there a few times. Always had a good time."

"I'm sure you did." She's still cupping the bourbon glass between her fingers, as though trying to warm herself on the fiery liquid.

"What's that supposed to mean?" If I'm being kind to her, she can at least return the favor and not make assumptions about my character—though I do get what she means. When I say I had a good time in P-town, I really mean I had a good time.

"Nothing. I don't know. I don't actually know you all that well, Ali. Thank you for taking me in tonight. I didn't want to stay for dinner, but I didn't really feel like returning to an empty, sparsely-furnished apartment either." She glances around. "I like your place. It has a warmth to it."

"I have a spare room. You can stay if you like. I can even throw in some pancakes for breakfast." I can see she's hesitating, but I can also see she's not really one to instantly take to the kindness of strangers. Though I'm hardly still a stranger.

"Pancakes for breakfast, huh," she says in the end. "No matter how bad I feel, and in need of comfort food, I would never start my day with a sugar bomb like that. Though, lately, I've sure been sugar-loading in the evening." She takes another hefty sip from her glass, emptying it in the process. "I probably shouldn't have any more."

"I can get you some water." I'm beginning to feel the effect of the liquor as well. We did skip dinner, after all. "Are you hungry?"

"I lost my appetite a while ago, but I know I have to eat."

"I'll toss something together. I promise not to present you with a sugar bomb." I try to find her gaze, but she looks away.

"Thank you," she says with a sigh, and leans back in the sofa.

CHAPTER FOURTEEN

KATHERINE

Because I really don't want to go home, I'm still at Ali's as midnight approaches. She hasn't asked me to leave yet—she even asked me to stay, but I'm not sure I can do that. Sitting here with her in her living room already feels weird enough. In a way, it's both a blessing and a curse that I had to fall apart in front of her. She has surprised me with her kindness, and with the way she listens attentively, her head slanted to the side, her eyes oozing tenderness. She must be getting sick of me by now.

She made us a plate of spaghetti with leftover sauce from the freezer and it wasn't half bad. At least it soaked up some of the alcohol swarming my bloodstream, though when she offered me a glass of red wine after dinner, I didn't refuse, and I feel myself slowly entering that much softer state of mind that comes with drinking a nice red.

"One more question and then I'll go home," I say, finally finding the courage to look her in the eyes.

"Shoot, but, for the record, I think you should stay. It's not a nuisance, in case that's what you're thinking. I'd feel better knowing you're not alone tonight." Her voice is very soft. She has kicked off her shoes and is sitting in an arm chair with the sort of nonchalance I remember her displaying on stage. She's being so sweet to me right now, I don't want to ask her my question anymore.

"Truth be told, I don't feel much like going home. I don't even have a cat anymore." Felix didn't survive our relationship. My beloved cranky cat passed away two years ago. "It's hard when you've shared a place for so long. Even though my new place is much smaller than where we used to live together, it always feels too big, like there's too much space for just me."

"Stay," Ali says, her voice firm, but sympathetic.

"Thank you." God, she really is very easy on the eyes. It helps that she looks nothing like Susan. I remember Susan ogling her at the NYU reunion a few years ago. Maybe this should be my revenge. Sleep with Ali West then walk all around Brooklyn with her until we run into Susan and Phoebe. Nice thought, but I catalog it away as unfathomable.

"What was your question?" Ali glances at me from over the rim of her glass.

"I don't know if I still want to ask you." I don't mean to be coy. I genuinely don't know.

"Now that you've said that, you have no more choice in the matter. It would be rude not to ask me." She smiles a slow, crooked smile.

"Okay." I sit up a bit straighter. "Er, that time Grace and I saw you play at that bar in Brooklyn that has been closed for a long time now."

"Temptation," Ali offers, still with a smile on her face.

"Yes. When you bought me that drink and came up to me, were you flirting?" An instant blush betrays how uncomfortable my own question makes me feel. I should have stuck to my guns and not asked it.

Ali chuckles loudly. "That was a long time ago."

"I know. You don't have to answer." The blush on my cheeks is very persistent.

"It's okay, I don't mind. I actually remember that night and… sometimes even wonder what would have happened if Grace hadn't returned from the bathroom when she did." She shoots me another kind of smile now. One I have no clue what to do with in the state I'm in. "The answer is yes, Katherine. I was flirting with you. I was still very much in my party days back then, and I thought it would be fun."

"I—er, just always believed you never liked me very much."

"Well, you never gave me a lot of reason to like you, which is why I thought it would be fun if I could get *you* to like *me*." Another smile.

"How brazen."

"That's me."

"I'm strangely flattered that you, er, would have even considered it." What? What do I mean by that? This is getting embarrassing. I rack my brain, more than eager for a swift change of subject, though I have no one but myself to blame for bringing this up.

"Why wouldn't I? You're a beautiful woman."

"And that's all it takes?" Argh, I can't seem to stop myself from engaging with Ali about this. Maybe because I'm interested in what else she has to say about it. Maybe she *could* be my rebound person. I get the distinct impression that she wouldn't say no. She has, after all, already persuaded me to stay the night.

"Why not? What's wrong with making love to a beautiful woman?"

"Making love? How can you make love to someone you barely know?"

"I've never had any problem with that." Ali has a grin on her lips, like no question I throw at her will faze her.

"I don't know. Some things are just beyond me, I guess." My thoughts are losing steam. I think I'm about ready for bed.

"I could ask you why, but I won't. Not tonight. How about we hit the hay?" She puts her glass down and stretches her arms above her head. I must have worn her out with all my talk of heartbreak. But at least she got my mind off Susan for a little while, which is more than I get most days.

"Thank you again. For everything." I push myself up, and my head spins a little.

"The bathroom is just through there. Middle door. I'll have something for you to sleep in ready on your bed when you get out. Water's in the kitchen. I can lend you a fresh pair of panties in the morning." Another grin.

"You really are the hostess with the mostest," I joke, and I'm surprised at my ability to do so.

"Always." She rises from her seat and, in walking past me, gives me a quick squeeze of the upper arm. "Good night, Katherine. I hope you get some sleep."

ALI

"Katherine? Are you awake?" It's past ten thirty and she still hasn't emerged from my guest room. I know she hasn't sneaked out in the middle of the night because her blazer is still draped over the back of a chair in the living room. I knock gently. Once, twice. No reply. So I open the door.

"Katherine?" She's lying sprawled out in the middle of the bed, the duvet half kicked off her, the t-shirt I loaned her only covering part of her belly. Still no response. "Katherine," I repeat and shuffle a little closer. I don't want to scare her by rudely waking her. I glance at the nightstand and see a bottle of Ambien. That's why she's still so out of it. I ponder letting her sleep longer, but hazard a guess that she'd want to be woken up not too late. I sit down on the edge of the bed and gently shake her arm.

Slowly, her eyes open. She blinks a few times, probably until I come into focus, then abruptly pulls the duvet over her body.

"Morning, Sleeping Beauty. I thought you'd want to catch some daylight today, so I woke you." I shoot her a big smile. "It's almost eleven."

"What?" Her eyes flit from here to there. "I couldn't get to sleep last night and I took a sleeping pill when it was already after two."

"At least you got some sleep. That's good." She looks so defenseless, so not put together. She also looks pretty amazing for someone who drank what she did last night and just woke from Ambien-induced sleep.

"Did you make pancakes?" She smiles when she says it.

"Not yet. I was waiting for you to get your lazy ass out of bed." I narrow my eyes. "And now you *will* start your day with a sugar bomb?"

"Thank you for letting me stay, Ali. It really made a difference. It stopped me from pacing around in the middle of the night, though I was tempted to scour your liquor cabinet at one point."

"Have you tried yoga?"

She looks at me as if I've just asked her whether she's tried heroin. "Once, but it's not really for me."

"I go to a class near your office a couple of times a week. You should consider it. It can really help."

"Help with what?" She pushes herself up a bit.

"With not having to take these to get to sleep at night." I grab the pill bottle from the nightstand.

"I don't always take them, but lately, I... I just haven't been able to sleep very well."

"I'm not judging, nor telling you what to do. I'm just suggesting you try something else. Something that doesn't involve putting pharmaceuticals in your body."

"I wouldn't normally," she stammers.

"Hey, I know." Inadvertently, I put my hand on her naked arm. We both stare at it. "It's fine." Because it feels somehow inappropriate for me to have my hand on her arm, I abruptly retreat.

"I'll consider it," she says, her voice a bit shaky.

"Feel free to shower while I prepare your breakfast deluxe." I'm back on my feet. "I found a brand new pair of underwear so you can use that if you like. Otherwise, I hear going commando is all the rage these days." I can't help it, before leaving the room, I shoot her a quick wink.

★ ★ ★

"These are amazing," Katherine says after she's taken a few bites. Then both our cellphones start ringing at the same time.

"It's Anna," I say.

"And what a surprise, it's Grace," Katherine says.

We both pick up.

"I'm sorry for not checking in last night, Ali," Anna says. "How's Katherine?"

"She's having breakfast as we speak and seems to be enjoying it greatly," I reply, knowing exactly what that sounds like.

"She's, er, what? She's at your place? She is?" Anna's voice goes up. "You… and her? You didn't?"

"Didn't what?" This is such fun.

"Did you… seduce her?" Anna asks, her voice having gone an entire octave higher in pitch.

"Why would you think that, dearest friend?" I glance at Katherine. I can't hear what she's saying, but her conversation seems to be more serious.

"Are you pulling my leg? What happened?" Anna sounds impatient now.

"She stayed in your old room, Anna. No need to get your panties in a wad."

"You had me wondering there for a minute." She laughs into the phone. "But is she okay?"

"Well, you know, she got her chest ripped open and her heart torn out. Things like that take some time to heal, we all know that. But I'm sure she'll be fine in the end."

"Okay, give her my love and tell her I wish we could have met under better circumstances."

"Will do." We hang up and I look at Katherine again. She's still talking to Grace, but she has her back turned to me. A few minutes later she hangs up.

"For a second, Anna actually believed we'd spent the night together," I say with a chuckle.

Katherine looks at me but doesn't say anything.

"What?" I'm no longer letting her off the hook.

"Well, you know, it must be because of your reputation." Her eyes sparkle a little, which is good to see.

"How dare you speak to me like that in my own home, and *after* I made you pancakes," I say with mock-indignation. I also couldn't care less about my reputation, though I do seem to care a little what Katherine thinks of me.

"In all earnestness, Ali, what can I do to thank you for last night and this morning? I'm not one to let that slide without giving something back. How about I treat you to dinner in a few weeks, when I feel more ready to leave my apartment again?"

"How about instead you join me for yoga this Wednesday. 8 p.m. Give me your number and I'll text you the address."

"Really?" She stabs at a pancake while looking at me incredulously.

"Why not try? It won't do you any harm, and who knows, you might even like it. I guarantee you'll sleep like a baby that night."

Slowly, she starts nodding. "Deal," she says.

CHAPTER FIFTEEN

KATHERINE

As soon as I got to the office on Monday I asked my assistant Jane, an avid yogi, what I needed to attend a yoga class. She gave me a quizzical look, as though she couldn't picture me on a yoga mat at all—I had trouble imagining it myself—then told me to just wear comfortable clothes and check beforehand if the studio provided mats.

On Wednesday, reeling from a budget meeting with the CEO and all the VPs, I make it to the studio with seven minutes to spare. Ali's already there and, bless her, has saved me a spot next to her. The only issue I have with it is that it's in the front row.

As though she can read my mind, she says, "I know beginners have a tendency to want to hide in the back, but it's hard to see properly from there. This is a much better spot." She's dressed in a floral top and loud hot-pink yoga pants.

I can only nod my obedience. Though I would have preferred not to have a bunch of people stare at my posterior.

The instructor walks in and sits down right in front of me. He smiles and I smile back, feeling very uneasy. The only other yoga class I ever took was a private one, years ago when I still had a personal trainer and he recommended one of his friends who was just starting out. It was an embarrassing experience from start to finish, I remember now, and I'm beginning to wonder what I'm doing here. What did Ali put on those pancakes last Sunday to have me so easily agree to do this? I'm the exact opposite of a yoga person. I'm not bendy and not spiritual and, truth be told, my workout regimen has suffered from being in a long-term relationship. A fact I only just recently realized. Me, the person who used to deride couples for giving up on their healthy routines so easily once they found the comfort of a relationship.

"Do we have any newcomers this evening?" the instructor asks. "Please raise your hand if you're new."

I lift up my hand and look around. No one else has their hand in the air. Great. I'll be the only one making a fool of myself then.

"What's your name, please?" he asks.

"Katherine."

"Very nice to meet you, Katherine. Don't worry about being a beginner. For every pose we do, I'll show you a modified version. If you feel uncomfortable with any pose, just go back to child's pose. Like this." He sits his ass on his heels, bends forward and stretches his arms in front of him. "Try to focus on your breath more than on holding a particular pose," he says, still face-down. Then he looks up. "Most of all, try to enjoy yourself. There's no room for self-consciousness in here, though I know it's hard to get rid of that in the beginning." He pushes himself up and stands in front of his mat. "Now let's start with taking a few deep breaths."

Turns out the actual yoga class was not the most awkward part of the evening. Afterwards, all class attendees, of which eighty percent are women, flock to the changing room. I've been in locker rooms before, of course, but never with so many people at once, and certainly not with Ali West peeling off her tight yoga clothes next to me.

"And?" she asks. "Do you feel zen?"

Admittedly, it wasn't as hard as I had anticipated—I modified most of my poses—and I do feel more relaxed than before I arrived. "I don't really know what zen feels like, but"—I glance around—"this is hardly a beneficial place for it."

Ali nods as though she gets it, but at the same time, in the most casual manner, pulls her top over her head and stands in front of me in just her bra. I suspect she doesn't even know what the word self-conscious means. "Tell you what. You take all the time you need in here and I'll wait for you in the lobby. We'll talk more then."

"Okay." I turn away to face my locker and busy myself with rummaging through my clothes unnecessarily. I try not to glance sideways when she undoes her bra and wait to move until she has a towel wrapped around herself.

After I've undressed in an intense exercise of locker room towel gymnastics—always trying to hide most of my body—and I've taken a shower, I wonder if Ali and I are friends now. I stayed in her guest room and we just did a yoga class together. That all does sound like something friends would do. I guess, friends or not, I will be seeing more of her now that Grace is so in love with Anna.

★ ★ ★

We're having a bite in the sister-restaurant of the yoga studio. I munch on quinoa and chia seeds and a bunch of vegetables, which, after the way I've been treating my body since the break-up, might just be what I need.

"I'd never have taken you for a health nut," I say to Ali, who has dressed in a very loose pair of pants and a hoodie. I'm back in my office clothes and it makes me feel like I'm her grandmother.

"I'm not." She glances at me from under her lashes. "I eat pancakes, remember? And I poured you half a bottle of bourbon the other night."

"True. You're actually a bad influence." I give a chuckle.

"How do you feel?"

I take a second to think. "Better, or at least a bit more human again. All that deep breathing must have been good for me."

"Excellent." Ali keeps looking at me. "Join me again next week?"

"I'll need to check my schedule." I take a sip from my spinach-celery juice.

"Or you could schedule around it," Ali offers.

She seems keen to see me again. "Let me see what I can do." I pull my phone out of my bag and see that I'm free next Wednesday evening. "I'll be here."

"Good. I'll save you a mat in the front again." She throws in a big smile and, this time, as opposed to last Saturday, I can actually enjoy it.

ALI

I've organized a do-over of Anna and Grace's best friends meeting their love-interests by inviting them and Katherine to a gig. I only perform once or twice a month these days, but when I do, I give it my all—not that I've ever given any less than I possibly could on the stage.

On gig day, my vibe is always different, as though my body and my mind know to conserve energy and let me shine after dark. I start my set with "Closer to Fine" which, since I started playing it with the kids all the time, is no longer a lesbian anthem in my mind, but for this crowd tonight it sure still is.

To my surprise, Katherine has become a regular at yoga on Wednesday evenings. She seems to have really taken to it, and I'm glad for her. We've struck up a kind of friendship, meeting once a week. She tells me about her day and I tell her about mine. I know she tries to avoid the Susan subject, but it sometimes slips into conversation, because how could it not? Katherine's pain is still so raw and, now that I've gotten to know her a little bit, she doesn't strike me as the kind of person to get over something like that quickly. She's a dweller.

I shoot her a few poignant glances during my set. She looks like she's enjoying it. Anna still hollers the way she used to after every song. When I end my set with "Anna Begins" for old times' sake, she nearly goes mental.

As I make my way off the stage and try to reach my friends, a young woman intercepts me.

"Ali," she says, addressing me as if she knows me. "I've been waiting for weeks for you to play another gig. It was worth the wait." She flashes me a wide smile—one that, a few years ago, I would have immediately accepted as an open invitation.

"Thank you." This girl must be mid-twenties, tops. I don't remember seeing her at any of my previous gigs, though I may pay less attention these days. "I appreciate that." Perhaps, because this is a tiny venue, she only just tonight scraped together the courage to approach me.

"Can I buy you a drink?" she asks, then stretches out her hand, "I'm Heather."

I'm reluctant to accept. Not only because it feels inappropriate, what with her being so young, but also because I can feel Anna, Grace and Katherine making eyes at me. "Pleased to meet you, Heather." I give her my best, non-seductive smile. "That's very nice of you to offer, but my friends over there"—I point at their table—"are waiting for me."

"Oh." She seems to deflate in front of me, and I feel so sorry for her, I backtrack.

"Okay, just a quick one, then."

"Yay!" A new life force seems to grab hold of her and she elbows us a way to the bar. Before following her, I shoot what I hope is a very apologetic look at the others. Anna will understand—and explain.

After Heather has ordered me a bottle of my favorite beer without having to ask me what I like, she holds out her phone. "Can we take a selfie?"

"Sure." I'm still riding high on post-gig adrenalin, on that warm glow of accomplishment riding through my veins, because that's the thing about singing in front of a crowd: it provides instant gratification. A two-way street of energy between me and the audience. I used to be addicted to it, I see now, but when I reached my mid-thirties, I had to accept that my body simply wasn't willing anymore to stay up late several times a week. I have to get up early these days to run the Music For The Children foundation. I have to hand it to my mother, she played that hand well.

I look into Heather's phone camera and, behind it, catch a glimpse of Katherine, who is eyeing me with a very disapproving expression on her face—as if, instead of merely having my picture taken with Heather, I'm making out with her.

"Cheers." I clink my beer bottle against Heather's and make some meaningless conversation. I've never had a problem chatting with strangers after a gig and often considered being able to do so a laudable quality, but it feels different with Shepherd's judging glance on me. I'm also not one to ditch my friends for too long. I quickly down the beer, thank Heather for it profusely, and say my goodbyes to her.

"Made plans for later?" Anna says as soon as I arrive at their table. "For when us oldies have left the premises?" She has one arm draped around Grace's shoulder, and I can't help but wonder how that made Katherine feel.

"I have to be nice to my fans."

"Ali is always *very* nice to her fans, especially the good-looking ones," Anna explains to Grace.

"Hey, this could easily have been us in college." I change the subject. "Four NYU girls in a bar, having a good time."

"Yeah right," Katherine says. "Like we got along so well back then."

I lock my gaze on her. Her skin looks better these days. She has started taking better care of herself again. Most of the post-break-up self-pity has gone. "Under different circumstances, who knows what could have happened?"

"She's right, Katie," Grace says. "We were four out lesbians going to the same college. It's a miracle that our paths *didn't* cross."

"But they did," Katherine says. "And I'm fairly certain Ali and I, even under different, very favorable circumstances, would never have been friends. We're just too different."

I want to ask what's eating Katherine tonight. We've been hanging out for a couple of months now. I thought we were long past all that college stuff. Maybe she's a bit miffed because I left her alone in the company of the two obnoxious lovebirds too long. "We're all friends now. That's what matters most." I try to hold her gaze, but she looks away. Maybe I'll have to make her pancakes again some day soon.

"Did that girl give you her number?" Grace asks.

"She wanted to, but I'm not interested." Though, of course, when a pretty woman hits on me, there's always a tiny flicker of interest, even if it's just the sensation of being flattered. "She's so young."

"And that's the only reason?" Katherine asks with a definite edge to her tone.

I give her a hard look, but we're not that close yet that I would just question her about her attitude in front of Grace and Anna. We're still in the phase where we're getting to know each other better. Is she going to ruin it again? I don't reply and ask Anna what she thought of the new song I played.

While I listen to Anna and Grace discuss my songwriting skills, I can't help but wonder if Katherine's gone back to her former uptight ways because she's jealous. If she wasn't still so cut up about Susan, I'd consider it a possibility.

CHAPTER SIXTEEN

KATHERINE

Over the months, I've upped my yoga practice from once to two or three times a week. Yoga has really forged a bond between Ali and me, and this Saturday afternoon, she has taken me to a new yoga studio we were both eager to try out after someone at work told her about it. I can't stand on my head yet the way she does, but I've learned not to rush, to progress at a natural pace and, I guess, that's what I've taken away from regular yoga practice the most. Taking time to breathe and do the opposite of rush.

With Anna being her best friend and Grace being mine, we often see each other on social occasions as well, because Anna and Grace have vowed to not become one of those lesbian couples who always stay in and never see their friends anymore just because they've found love. They have, however, already moved in with each other.

"I need something deliciously sinful after that," Ali says when we exit the studio. Maybe because it's Saturday afternoon, she's not dressed in her usual post-yoga lounge wear. She looks good in those skinny jeans, although at times I catch myself thinking that a woman of nearly forty shouldn't be wearing jeans that tight anymore.

"I might know just the place," I say without thinking. "They have the most glorious triple chocolate cake you've ever tasted."

"Take me there at once." Ali puts some desperation in her voice.

"Okay, but just so you know, I haven't been there in a good long while because…" Argh, I hadn't wanted to pause. "Well, Susan and I used to go there. It was kind of one of our *spots*."

Ali stops walking. "This will be good for you then. Time to exorcize Susan from the place and make a new memory there. Override her lingering presence there in your brain." She starts walking again, then turns around. "Which way?"

Once we reach Chocolate Heaven, Ali says, "Subtly named, I like that."

"Save your snark and prepare to be amazed."

"Let me just have a closer look into this window to postpone my climax a little longer." She bends over to examine the cakes on display and runs her tongue over her lips in an exaggerated fashion. Then she straightens her posture and puts a hand on my shoulder. "Ready?" she asks.

"Yes."

Then I hear someone clear their throat behind me and say, "Katherine?"

It's Susan.

I turn around and discover it's not just Susan. It's Phoebe as well. I've never actually met Phoebe, but I did google her profusely, just to try and find out why she was so much better than me. Ali's hand slips off my shoulder.

Susan cocks her head. "Are you, er… that singer from the NYU reunion?" she asks Ali.

"The one and only." Ali does her trademark head tilt and, without giving it any further thought, I grab her hand and wrap my fingers around it.

Susan notices and her eyes widen. "Are the two of you… together?"

I don't give myself any further time to consider this and just say, "Yes."

I feel the grip of Ali's fingers tighten around mine. She leans in to me a little. "It came as a bit of surprise, but here we are," she adds.

I could kiss her right now, though I do feel a familiar blush creep up my cheeks. I'm not sure how long I can keep up with this charade.

"I'm so happy for you, Katherine," Susan says. "I've been so worried about you."

As well you should have, I think. But I steel myself and, my fingers still firmly intertwined with Ali's, look at Phoebe. "You must be Phoebe." I manage to actually inject something saccharine into my voice.

"Very nice to meet you." She can't look me in the eyes. I derive a little bit of satisfaction from that fact, though it's only logical seeing as she stole my partner from me.

"Were you going in for some triple-choc cake?" Susan has started shuffling her weight around awkwardly. Neither one of us still wants to be standing here, confronted with our pasts and how things played out between us.

"Yes, but we can go somewhere else." At this point, I don't care anymore that I have to back down. I just want to get away from the two of them. My stomach no longer feels like ingesting a slice of overly rich cake either.

"No, no, Kat, please," Susan says, "we'll go. You stay." That must be the guilt speaking then. What does it feel like to leave your long-term partner for someone else? In the throes of our break-up, I wanted to ask her that question many times, but could never work up the nerve to hear the answer. Because what if she said it wasn't that hard?

"Come on." Ali tugs at my hand. "Let's go inside."

"It was good to see you, Katherine," Susan says. "Maybe we should get together some time." She doesn't say it, but I can almost hear her think it: now that you've found someone new as well.

"Yeah." I don't look back, just follow Ali into Chocolate Heaven.

Once inside, she frees her hand from my grasp and brings both her hands to my shoulders. "Are you okay?"

"Yeah, just, it was…" I stammer.

"Do you want something stronger than chocolate cake?" Ali wears her most friendly smile. I'm so happy she was by my side for this encounter.

"No." I shake my head vigorously. "Let's expel the ghost of Susan."

After we've placed our order and sat down, both of us picking at a huge piece of cake we've decided to share, I muster up the courage to say, "I'm sorry for, uh, grabbing your hand like that and making her think… you and I are a thing."

"It's fine. A stroke of genius, really." Ali has a crumb in the corner of her mouth, but I don't tell her. It amuses me and I could do with some amusement.

"I just… thought I was finally getting over her, you know? But then seeing them together. It's, er…" I run out of words, but not feelings. Bumping into them was a brutal reminder of how much she hurt me, of the most painful time of my entire life when the woman I believed I'd grow old with told me she loved someone else. When she ripped our world apart with just a few words. Even though I tried to appeal to our history and the life we had built and the love we had shared, I knew from the very beginning that there's no competing with new love.

"I get it, but don't let it ruin your day." Ali glances at me from under her long lashes. "You've been doing so well. I can so clearly see the change in you. Don't let her take that away from you. She has taken enough." She heaps some cake onto her fork. "Here. Have this instead." She brings the fork in front of my mouth. "Open wide." When I don't oblige, she says, "what if they're still outside the window, looking in? We'd better play our parts." She gives a breathy chuckle. "Come on, lover, open wide."

Then I do. I let Ali West feed me chocolate cake, the

way I let Susan a few months ago. Though I know the cake is in fact moist and delicious, it tastes dry and stale in my mouth.

ALI

"She pretended you were together?" Anna asks, her eyes wide.

"I applauded her for it afterwards. That's some quick on-your-feet thinking." Anna and I are having after-work drinks, just the two of us.

"Well, yes, but still."

"Still what?" I try to predict what she's going to say next. I can sort of guess.

"She used you." I hadn't expected that. Anna is not the same anymore since she fell so hard for Grace. I have to remind her at times that I don't want her moving to New Jersey and disappearing from my life again for years on end.

"Used me? What are you talking about?" She's probably just pestering me, trying to get me to say things I don't want to say.

"I'm your best friend, Ali. You can be honest with me." She leans over the table a little. "Do you have feelings for her?"

I roll my eyes. "I knew it." I lean in close as well. "I bet you and Grace daydream about Katherine and me getting together all the time when you want to take a break from being overly lovey-dovey with each other."

Anna scoots back. "What's that supposed to mean?" There's an inflection of hurt in her voice.

"Nothing, just... don't go making assumptions about me."

"I hardly think I am." She stands her ground.

"Look, Anna, as much as you may dream of the four

of us double-dating, Katherine got very, very hurt." I vividly remember how she flinched when unexpectedly faced with the woman who broke her heart—and the woman responsible for it. "She's not looking for anything serious."

"I wasn't talking about Katherine, Ali. I was talking about you. Though what you just said gave away plenty. I rest my case."

"You've got the wrong idea." I lower my defenses a little. This is Anna, after all. I'm not being cross-examined by a detective specialized in matters of the heart. "I will freely admit to having wanted to flirt with her on occasion, but that was a long time ago. When I met her again after you and Grace got together, she was a wreck, and flirting with her hasn't entered my head since. If anything, it's a miracle that she and I are even friends, what with our history."

"But that's just the thing, though," Anna says. "You have become friends."

"A fact for which you should only be grateful. Instead of nosey."

"All right. I'll back off, but just tell me one more thing. How did it make you feel when she pretended to be your girlfriend?"

I chuckle. Anna will always find a way to get her point across, and to make me answer a question I had no intention of answering. "The only thing it made me feel, dear Anna, was happy to help out a friend."

She nods, as though my reply has finally left her satisfied. "Anything else to report from the more amorous sphere of your life? Any more phone numbers gathered? Any walks of shame?"

"There was this one woman," I begin, and tell her about a random encounter I had with the mother of one of the children I teach guitar to. I ran into her in the street and we got talking, went for a drink, and one thing led to another.

"Good to hear the old Ali West hasn't entirely checked

out," Anna says.

"It wasn't anything I wanted to pursue. Just a bit of fun."

"It's been a while since you pursued anything." Anna finishes her glass of wine.

"I guess I haven't met anyone pursue-worthy." I think it's time to change the subject to Anna. "But do tell me all the tiny details about your love life. And don't hold back on the mushy stuff. I can take it."

"Really?" Anna quirks up her eyebrows, as though she needs to ask for my permission to start raving about Grace again.

"Of course. What wonders has Grace performed in your life the past weeks?"

"Well, now that we've been living together for a few weeks, I think I can safely say she's the real love of my life. The memory of Grayson pales in comparison to her. She's just so… easy to be with."

I listen to Anna talk about Grace for a while longer, until she's interrupted by the arrival of a message on her phone—from Grace, of course.

While she replies, I think about what she asked me earlier. About Katherine. How did it really make me feel when she grabbed my hand in front of Susan? I can be honest with myself, though I hadn't bothered asking myself that question yet.

When we met for our regular Wednesday evening yoga class—which Katherine *always* makes time for in her busy work schedule—it was awkward for a minute or two, as though the hand-grabbing was still sort of hanging over us and we didn't really know how to deal with each other because of it. But then everything went back to normal and I assisted Katherine while she attempted her first headstand, which she's still a few months away from completing successfully. And that was that. She didn't even mention Susan or Phoebe. It was as if it had never happened.

As to how it actually made me feel to pretend Katherine and I were together, I guess the completely honest answer would be: not totally averse to it being real.

CHAPTER SEVENTEEN

KATHERINE

"Do you think I should start dating again?" I ask Grace. "Even if just to find out how it makes me feel?" I'm at her and Anna's place, waiting for Ali and Anna to return with take-out Chinese to sustain us through a lesbian cult movie night we're holding.

"How long has it been now?" She pours me some more wine.

"Nine months and seventeen days."

"If you're still counting in days, then you definitely need to do something. Have a rebound fuck or something."

"Grace, come on, you know that's not what I do."

"Have you perhaps considered it's something you never did *before,* but might be open to now? I don't want to push you if you're not ready, but… I've gotten inquiries about you."

My jaw slackens. "You have what?"

"Now you're back on the market, inquiring minds want to know. That's all."

"Whose inquiring mind?" I'm not sure if I should be flattered or offended by this. What kind of terminology is *being on the market* anyway to indicate someone is single?

"Friends of friends with single acquaintances." Grace plays with the stem of her wine glass. "Believe it or not, Katie, you're a catch. Of course, I already knew that when we were in college, when you so cold-heartedly dumped me, but now word is spreading and... my guess is you won't be single for too long. If that's what you want, of course."

The front door opens, giving me some time to ponder this. Ali and Anna walk in with food containers.

It has become comfortable between the four of us. So comfortable, in fact, that, along with Grace and Anna, I should count my lucky stars as well for the two of them falling in love and involving me in this close-knit circle of four—despite the fact that I crumbled at the first sight of their fresh love. But now that I'm past that, it's so much fun to spend a Saturday evening like this, the four of us huddled up on the couch, just feeling warm and fuzzy in the embrace of our friendship. A friendship that has been so instrumental in me getting over Susan.

"Which one first? *Desert Hearts* or *When Night Is Falling*?" Ali asks.

"Chances are Anna will fall asleep during the first one, so she should decide," Grace says.

"I will do no such thing." Anna swats Grace playfully on the thigh.

"I like both and I'll stay awake, so either one is fine with me." Despite having owned both movies on DVD for years, I haven't seen either for a long time. I do, however, remember the vivid sex scenes in both films, and wonder how they will make me feel. Because one of the worst consequences of breaking up with someone, is the lack of touch that follows. Grace hugs me more frequently than before, and grabbing hold of Ali's hand that day we ran into Susan and Phoebe did, in hindsight, create a bit of a jolt to run through my untouched system, but it's hardly enough. A gentle caress from a friend is nowhere near as powerful as even the briefest hug from a lover.

"Let's eat first," Ali says. "You don't want chicken chow mein all over your brand new sofa."

Once we're all seated and delving into the food, I say to

Grace, "Who has inquired about me?" We're all friends now. I can ask Grace in front of Anna and Ali.

"Inquired about what?" Ali asks.

Grace addresses us both. "Katherine here is a prime piece of meat that is new to the market." There she goes with her dreadful analogy again. "Before you arrived with the food she wondered if she should start dating again. Put two and two together…" Grace holds her fork in the air triumphantly as though she's just made a significant scientific discovery. "If you want my opinion, I think that, yes, you should start dating again." She looks straight at me now. "I hear Orla O'Neill wants to take you out."

"Who the hell is Orla O'Neill and how does she know me?"

"A friend of a friend—of Irish descent, as you might have guessed," Grace says. "She's a big shot at KPMG and she's had professional dealings with you. When she heard about your break-up, she showed a keen interest."

"Do you want me to google her?" Anna asks. She must be keen as well, as she's already holding her phone.

"I may know someone as well," Ali says.

The three of us go silent and stare at her. For a split second, the thought flits through my mind that she'll suggest herself.

"Music For The Children's brand new part-time accountant, Greta. When I met her a few weeks ago I immediately thought of you, Katherine. She reminds me of you so much. I think you'd have a lot in common, bar the fact that she works for a non-profit, but there has to be some contrast." Ali says this as though she's got it all figured out. A tiny part of me is disappointed that she didn't propose herself. Though I am slightly intrigued by Greta.

ALI

"The more I get to know Greta, the more perfect I think she is for you," I say. "She went through a pretty nasty break-up a while ago as well. The only possible obstacle I can see is that there's a child in the mix. A girl. Ten years old, I think. But…" I hold up my hand and reach for my phone with my other. I scroll around until I find the picture on the MFTC Facebook page I'm looking for. "Look at this." I give Katherine the phone.

"Just so as to not forget about the case I was making," Grace taps feverishly on her own phone, "my candidate has actually asked about you, Katherine." She gives me a quick glare. I guess it's a competition now. Fine. I'm always up for a silly bout of sparring.

"Here, Katie," Grace says and hands over her phone.

"Jesus," Katherine says. "Am I really so horrible at being single that you all want to pawn me off as soon as possible?"

"It's nice to have options," Anna says.

"Why don't you set Ali up on a date as well? She's single, and I'm sure plenty more inquiring minds want to know about her." Katherine looks at me. Her glance has some defiance in it. But I think she's also sort of flattered by all of this, though possibly scared stiff.

"Oh, no," Anna is quick to say. "No blind dates for Ali. She likes to pick her own women. And she gets plenty." Anna blows me a kiss.

Katherine turns to me. "Do you? Get plenty?" There's something in her glance I can't identify.

I shrug. "Sure, although that would depend on your definition of plenty." I have to smile because I can so easily predict this is going to wind her up.

"So, what are we talking about here? One woman a

month, or a week?" She seems genuinely interested to find out.

I steeple my fingers and look at her. "Not every month or week is the same. It varies and a lot depends on what I've got going on. But, you know, when I have a gig I usually have options."

"Options?" While what I'm saying is close enough to the truth, I could have chosen to phrase it differently so as not to get under Katherine's skin. But I know what gets her riled up and it's so delicious to watch when it happens. "When was the last time you, er, you know?"

"I you-know what?" I shoot Grace a quick glance and she has a grin on her face.

"Well, you know... you, huh, had sex." Katherine's cheeks flush in the most adorable way possible. I'm not entirely sure she's ready for a blind date, though.

"Hm." I pretend to rack my brain, though of course I remember. "About two weeks ago."

Katherine just looks at me and doesn't say anything.

"What?"

"When and with whom?" Her gaze is pinned on me. I guess she really, really wants to know.

"Why so interested?"

"I'm sorry." She shakes her head. "It's really not my place to ask."

"I'm curious too," Grace says, earning her a quizzical sideways glance from Anna.

"What does it matter? And how did we get talking about this? Weren't we trying to decide who to send Katherine on a blind date with?"

"How many women have you actually slept with?" Katherine asks.

Ah, the big question. I shake my head and chuckle. "What does it matter?" I repeat.

"It—it doesn't." I bet she's regretting her spontaneous question already. Judging by how crimson her neck is, she is.

That question must have been on the tip of her tongue for a while though, for her to blurt it out like that.

"No offense, Ali," Anna says. "You know I say this with love, but I bet you don't even know."

"As I just said, what does it even matter? I have a healthy sexual appetite of which I'm not ashamed. I had a lot of one-night stands in my day and I still have the occasional one now. Why wouldn't I? I'm single and well, I guess I'm just not a vibrator-only kind of girl."

"Hear, hear!" Grace is actually clapping.

Katherine looks at her but I can't see what that look is supposed to convey. Perhaps what I just said put Katherine off me much more than what she witnessed when we first met.

"Anyway, back to the subject at hand." I try to look at Katherine, but, for some reason, she can't meet my gaze. "Who's it going to be? My girl Greta, or Anna's friend of a friend Orla?"

"You know what? Let's just drop it. I appreciate the effort and all that, but I need to think about it." Whereas Katherine was comfortably sitting next to me earlier, her elbow occasionally bumping into mine while she ate, she now seems to shrink away from me.

All this time we were becoming friends I had believed she'd stopped judging me.

"Let's watch *When Night Is Falling* first," Anna says. "That's my favorite."

With that, the topics of blind dates and one-night stands have been officially closed for the night.

CHAPTER EIGHTEEN

KATHERINE

In the end, I based my decision purely on appearance. I'd like to think that I chose Greta over Orla because clearly Ali knew her better than Grace did Orla, but, if I'm truly being honest with myself, the reason why I'm sitting across from Greta instead of Orla is because her lips looked so delicious in that picture, and her eyes seemed piercing enough to look straight into my soul.

So here I am, on a blind date with a woman scouted for me by Ali. I'm so nervous I nearly knocked over my wine glass earlier, an affliction Greta seems to be suffering from as well.

"I'm not very good at this dating game," I say, sounding so very lame.

"Don't worry, neither am I." Greta is definitely attractive, but I feel so ill at ease, I have no idea what to say to her.

"So, what has Ali said about me?" I ask, because it might be a good conversation starter, and I'm also dying to know.

"Not that much. You know Ali. She likes to have that whole mysterious vibe going. She only said I wouldn't be disappointed. That she knows you well and, for one thing, you have your heart in the right place, though it did get stomped on severely a while back." Greta is very eloquent all of a sudden. Perhaps she's already chased off that first bout of nerves. I haven't.

So that's what Ali said about me. I have my heart in the right place. How's that for being vague.

"I don't have much more information about you, except that you work with her and that you have a child," I blurt out.

We chit-chat over drinks, then move on to dinner and, inadvertently, the conversation keeps coming back to the one thing we have in common: Ali.

"What's it like working with her?" I ask.

"Technically, I work *for* her," Greta says. "She hired me." She smiles broadly. "She's by far the easiest boss I've ever had. She trusted me from the very beginning, said she knew I was trustworthy otherwise she wouldn't have hired me. And she's great with the kids. She's pretty awesome, actually. How do you know her?"

"Our respective best friends are in a relationship." I don't feel like dragging up the whole college story again. "So we've ended up seeing quite a bit of each other. We go to yoga together on Wednesdays."

"Oh yeah, Ali's been trying to persuade me to come, but it's difficult with Erin. It's hard to get away from home in the evening." She glances at her phone. "Sorry that I keep checking my messages, by the way."

I shake my head. "I understand." For some reason, the fact that Ali asked Greta to join her for yoga grates on my nerves a little. Perhaps it's a silly thought, but I believed doing yoga together was *our* thing, though I soon realize how stupid that thought actually is.

When Greta has turned her attention fully back to me, she sips from her wine, then asks, "So you and Ali don't have a romantic history? I'm only asking because with lesbians you just never know." She beams me a smile. Her mouth is wide and her lips full.

"Me and Ali?" I shake my head. "No way. Never."

Greta leans back a bit. "I wasn't expecting such fervor. I mean, she is a very attractive woman."

Then it dawns on me and I just have to ask. "You and her?" I feel as though I don't even have to ask the question anymore. Knowing Ali equals knowing the answer.

"What?" Greta chuckles. "I'm aware she has a bit of a reputation, but at work she's very professional. She wouldn't do that. Especially because she's the boss."

Oh. Perhaps I am too quick to judge sometimes. "We have a bit of a weird history, Ali and I," I hear myself say. I glance up at Greta, at those luscious lips of hers, and her inviting, wide eyes, and realize that, for the most part of our date, we've only talked about Ali West. I also realize that I don't mind that at all. I like talking about Ali; I like finding out more about her—I even liked having my theory about her disproved. Then it hits me. *Oh shit.*

I like Ali.

Through dessert, I try not to talk about Ali. I also try not to think about her but that only causes the opposite reaction in my brain. As long as I'm sitting across from Greta, Ali is all I can think about. Perhaps the thought has been there in the back of my mind all along. Perhaps doing yoga together with Ali is the main reason why I like it so much. And I'm on this date with the woman she picked precisely because she chose her for me.

But Ali and I are friends. Really good friends by now. She's a friend I can't afford to lose.

Instead of questioning Greta about work and other subjects that could lead back to Ali, I ask her about her daughter and her life before she became single again. Ali was right. We do have a lot in common.

Long past dessert we compare stories of running into our exes, of finding a bracelet or a long-forgotten card that reminds us of better times. By the end of the night, I do feel a kinship with her, but I'm no longer sure I want to kiss her voluptuous lips. Not that I would kiss her on the first date anyway.

"Do you want to do this again sometime?" she asks when we're outside the restaurant. "It was nice to meet a kindred spirit."

"I have your number," I say. "I'll call you."

"If I don't call you first." She leans in a little and we kiss each other on the cheek.

In the taxi on the way home, all I can think of is Ali.

ALI

"Someone walked into the office with a wide grin on her face this morning." All throughout yoga class, I've been waiting to spring that line on Katherine, knowing full well it would make her blush like a schoolgirl. Katherine and I are having our habitual post-yoga meal and juice, and I look at her expectantly, but she doesn't say anything.

"You didn't like her?" I could have been horribly wrong about putting the two of them together, of course. You just never know for sure how two people are going to gel until they actually meet.

"I do. I did. She's such a nice woman." Katherine looks pained.

"But…"

"I don't know, Ali. I can't really explain it. The best I can come up with is that it was, in fact, still too soon."

"Really? It's been almost a year."

"So." She shrugs. "They say it takes half the time you were together to fully get over someone."

"They might say that," I make my voice sound as gentle as I can get it, "but I'll be damned if I'm going to see you moping around for another four years."

"I just got the distinct impression she was looking for

something serious and I don't think I'm the person to give her that." Katherine's not making much sense tonight. If she said that Greta had done something that really put her off, or they hadn't gotten along at all, I would get it, but this sort of reluctance I don't understand.

"So what do you want? A fling?"

"Look, it was just a test, okay? I didn't make any commitments. I was just testing the waters to see if I was ready and it turns out I'm not. Give me a break."

"Whoa." I drop my fork. "Will you please tell me what's really going on here?"

"Nothing's going on. Just stop... pestering me."

"Katherine," I whisper. "You're clearly upset. Did Greta say or do anything to have that effect on you?"

"No. It's all me. I'm too damaged now. She's a perfectly nice woman. Very attractive at that. But I just couldn't... see it."

"She might be open to a fling. It doesn't have to be serious. If you're very clear about what you want beforehand, no feelings will get hurt."

"And you'd know all about that, wouldn't you?" There's so much bite to Katherine's tone, I'm beginning to think I did something wrong.

"What's that supposed to mean?"

"Well, you know. You and all your one-night stands. You must have the protocol down to a tee."

"I fail to see what that has to do with how you feel about your date?"

"It doesn't have anything to do with it. I'm just confused and upset, I guess, for not being able to give Greta a better chance. And... I don't know." She expels a deep sigh.

"It's perfectly fine. You went on one date. She'll understand. No need to get so worked up about it. We're all different and we all process grief in our own way."

"I've never had a one-night stand," Katherine says.

"What's it like to just walk out of someone's door in the morning and never speak to them again after being so… intimate?"

"Why are you giving me the third degree about one-night stands all of a sudden?"

"Because you're the expert, obviously."

"Okay, look." I push my plate away from me entirely, having lost my appetite. "If you want to sit here and insult me for a while, fine, be my guest, but at least do me the courtesy of telling me why you're so upset with me."

"I'm sorry." Her gaze flits from here to there. "I promise you that I'm not upset with you, just with myself. I guess that going on this date triggered some memories. I don't know." She lets her chin fall onto her upturned palms. "I really don't know what's going on with me today. I'm sorry for taking it out on you."

I think I may have an inkling of what Katherine needs. "Do you trust me?"

"What?"

Granted, my question has come a bit out of left-field.

"I want to take you somewhere. The kind of place where I would expect you to freak out a little, but I'm taking you there for a good reason. That's why I need you to trust me."

She cocks her head, narrows her eyes. "What do you have up your sleeve?"

"Come with me and find out."

I ask the cabbie to drop us off right in front of the store. Instantly, Katherine starts stammering.

"Are—are you kidding me?" She looks at me incredulously.

"I'm deadly serious." I haul her out of the cab and tug her inside by the hand.

"What are you implying?" She stands awkwardly by the door, her gaze skittering around.

I lean in close and find her ear. "I think that, in the absence of a partner or the prospect of a truly satisfying one-night stand, you need to take matters into your own hands, Katherine."

She laughs and shakes her head. "You are just unbelievable."

"I'm a good friend, is what I am. I'm always looking out for you... and you seemed a little tense. I bet you don't own a decent vibrator."

"That just goes to show you don't know as much about me as you think you do." She's getting sassy on me. I like it. "You could have just asked and it would have saved you a taxi ride."

"The look on your face when we arrived was well worth the cab fare."

A woman approaches us. "Can I help you ladies with anything tonight?"

I let Katherine reply. To my surprise, she says, "My friend here thinks I'm in need of a vibrator to help with my uptightness. Do you have any recommendations?" Katherine keeps her expression serious. Who knew she had this sort of reply in her? The thought flits through my head that, underneath that proper exterior of hers, she could very well be a wild one between the sheets. A shiver runs up my spine, but I shake it off.

"Of course," the woman says, and leads us to a counter where several models are displayed.

Katherine tries to keep up her bravado for as long as possible, but soon cracks appear, and no longer than ten minutes after we entered the shop, we're back outside on the sidewalk, each with a box clasped between our hands.

"I'm going to get you back for this," Katherine says and, finally, for the first time all night, looks me in the eyes.

"I look forward to that." I inch closer to kiss her goodnight.

It could be my imagination, but when her lips touch my

cheek, it feels as though she's lingering.

CHAPTER NINETEEN

KATHERINE

Thankfully, over the weekend, I don't see Anna, Grace or Ali. I don't know what to do with myself since I had that realization on my date with Greta, whom I have called up to say that even though I like her very much, I found myself not ready to take things further. I would never leave anyone hanging and not tell them what's what, not even if it hurt their feelings a little in the short term. Long-term thinking is, among other things, what I do for a living. I decide to take the long-term approach to my friendship with Ali.

Just to get out of my apartment, I go to work on Saturday, but instead of doing any actual work, I open a new Excel sheet with two columns. One column I call *pros*, the other *cons*.

In the pro column of telling Ali I have feelings for her, I only come up with: *We could possibly be happy, but there are no guarantees*, which is a half-hearted pro if I've ever seen one.

The cons column is filled with reasonable arguments for me to get over this as quickly as possible without telling anyone, because, and I have my well-developed long-term thinking muscle to thank for this, I absolutely do not want to jeopardize our friendship. Contrary to what I've believed about Ali West since I first met her, befriending her has been a very rewarding experience. She's kind, funny, talented and, unlike what I always thought, extremely reliable. Of course, she's also sexy, and sweet in a way that makes me think my feelings might be reciprocated if I tried, but these are not things I can focus on right now. These are not things that will save our friendship in the long run.

Because, despite the two of us becoming close friends, I can't convince myself that we would make a good couple. She doesn't even know how many women she has slept with. Ali might be very relaxed about that, but to me, such a thing is unfathomable. On top of that, she doesn't have the greatest track record with relationships, nor has she ever displayed any signs of wanting to be in one. We're too different. While I think it's actually our differences that make for our excellent friendship, a relationship is an entirely different kettle of fish.

By the time I leave my office, my mind is made up. Ali will never know. Even Grace and Anna will never know. The second I tell them they will just spur me on to follow my heart and so on, and I won't have any of that. I'm not about to risk another case of heartbreak for a chance with Ali, who couldn't be further removed from relationship material. No one will ever know, but me.

The only problem I foresee is that I will need some time to get my act together and to learn to behave normally around her while battling this infatuation. My outburst last Wednesday was a direct result of me wanting more from her than I could have, and of her setting me up with someone who wasn't her. I'm going to need some time away from her, which may look suspicious, but having the job that I have, I always have an excuse to cover my tracks. I'll be busy. I'll have work emergencies. I'll make it believable.

What's the alternative? I see two other possible outcomes involving some sort of short-term gratification. I could confess my feelings, she could reciprocate, and we could find out the hard way that Katherine Shepherd and Ali West are not meant to be together. Or, even worse, I could tell her, and she could not respond in kind. Our friendship wouldn't survive either scenario.

The only thing I can hope for at this point is that I get over her quickly.

✷ ✷ ✷

The following Wednesday I text Ali that I won't be able to make it to our yoga class, citing a work emergency. Five minutes after I've sent my text, she calls me.

"You never cancel yoga," she says, instead of hello. "It's the one thing every single week you do only for yourself and your sanity."

"I know, but today it's just not going to—"

"What could possibly be so important that you have to busy yourself with it at eight in the evening and can't wait until tomorrow?"

"Ali, please, you have no idea. My job comes with certain amounts of pressure and sacrifice."

"Are you sure?" She's persistent.

"Yes. You know I wouldn't cancel on a whim."

"Okay, but join me tomorrow for a class then."

Argh. "I can't make any promises. I have no idea just now how my schedule will evolve, but I promise you I will go to at least one class this week. Maybe I'll try to fit in a lunch time session tomorrow."

"Fair enough. Don't work too hard, okay? All my family does is work and I can assure you it's not worth it in the end."

"I promise." After we hang up, I'm faced with a fatal flaw in my plan.

I have to lie. It doesn't matter that it's not a big flagrant lie, and that I can easily stay in the office well past eight every evening and keep myself busy. A lie is a lie, and I don't lie.

I lean back in my office chair, feeling absolutely no desire to stay late tonight, but I have no choice. The yoga class we attend together is close to my office building and I might run into her. This is just ridiculous. Maybe I should just tell her and trust that our friendship is strong enough to withstand any outcome. In a way, having these feelings represents a small triumph after the heartbreak I suffered. Just the fact that a slew of butterflies flap their wings in my belly when I think of Ali, is a victory over the darkness that came after Susan. I can fall in love again. That sensation alone is enough to make me want to rush out of my office and attend yoga, not for relaxation purposes, but to see Ali.

I try to remember how long it's been all about Ali for me. If it wasn't for her, I'd probably still be mourning the demise of my relationship with Susan. Intentionally or not, she was there every step of the way. How gallantly she coaxed me to her apartment after my mini breakdown the first time we saw each other again. How easily she orchestrated that. No drama. No guilt. Just following her instincts.

And that night we all went to see her play and she got hit on by a twenty-something woman. I distinctly remember not being able to look away as she caught the young woman in her gaze, how she so obviously flirted back, because that's how she is. And how it made me feel. Jealous.

But, more than anything, I'm scared—petrified. While it's true she tried to seduce me that one night at Temptation, that was a very long time ago. Everything has changed. I must be strong. Katherine Shepherd doesn't foolishly declare her love for one of her friends and wait to see what happens next.

I turn my attention back to my computer screen and bury myself in work.

ALI

"Where's Katherine?" This is a big day for me and she knows it.

"I'm sorry, Ali, she called me this morning to say she wouldn't be able to make it," Grace says.

"She called *you* to say that?" I scan Grace's face, to see if her expression can explain to me what's been going on with Katherine lately. "She couldn't have called me directly?"

"She knew you were busy rehearsing. She probably didn't want to bother you," Anna chimes in.

"I'm starting to get the very distinct impression she's avoiding me." I glance around the room; it's starting to fill up. Clayton and Denise have just arrived. "Anyway, I don't have time to deal with this right now."

"Good luck," Anna says.

"Thanks." I give her a quick nod. Today is a special day for the Music For The Children foundation, founded by my mother to lure me into getting a real job. It worked. I started out just teaching the enrolled kids a few guitar chords and practicing some harmonies, but today, to celebrate many years of fruitful work, we're putting on a full-on concert. These days, I also do much more than teach music, though I never really saw myself as a teacher, more as a music enthusiast who wants to share the love and pure joy of music with as many people as possible.

Katherine knows how important this afternoon is for me. I asked her to mark her calendar two months ago, just as I asked Grace, Anna and Jen, who are all present. My three siblings are here, with all their significant others and children, and of course my parents are in attendance as well. I haven't seen my dad beam with pride so much for his youngest since the day I graduated from NYU.

This isn't the first time Katherine has ditched me lately either. I've barely seen her, what with her coming up with a different excuse every week—though always work-related so to me they all sound the same.

When I text her, I only get back a curt reply a day later, or a few hours if I'm lucky. When I call, she rarely picks up. I can only conclude I have greatly offended her in some way, because no one suddenly becomes this busy at work—especially not on a Sunday afternoon like today. But I've been focusing on the kids and getting them ready for this gig. Frankly, Katherine Shepherd can go fuck herself.

✳ ✳ ✳

During the afternoon's big finale, a highly emotional rendition of "Closer To Fine" with the boys' voices harmonizing with the girls', and despite having been able to push her absence to the back of my mind all evening, Katherine slips back into my consciousness. Did taking her to that sex shop freak her out so much? Or was it the date she went on with Greta? Has it made her retreat back into seclusion? If so, why?

Darren, a seven-year-old boy with the most angelic voice, starts his solo of singing the chorus before the group joins in again, and the beauty of his voice hits me straight in the stomach, as though it's the culmination of all the gorgeous performances *my* kids delivered tonight. For them to be able to express themselves like this, while they get back this incredible energy from the audience, fills my eyes with tears for a brief moment.

Apart from Katherine's absence, this afternoon has been perfect. It didn't matter that little Ayla forgot the lyrics to "Up Where We Belong" and that both Gregory and Jason failed to have their guitars tuned before going on stage. The perfection we strived for tonight is of a different kind. I always tell the kids that they'll know when it's good because they will feel it—there's just no other way to qualify it—and I'm sure today they felt it.

Then I see her. In the back, the door opens and someone walks in. It's Katherine. Just in time for the encores. I don't feel disappointed anymore. I'm angry. I consider myself a pretty easy-going person, but her abandonment of our friendship angers me because it hurts. Because it happened without any explanation—as if she had suddenly decided to not need my friendship anymore. I don't have unreasonable expectations of my friends, but I do demand respect. Katherine has proven to be highly disrespectful of me and the bond we have.

After they've taken a bow, I guide the kids off the stage to a loud roar from the audience. I wouldn't expect any less noise even if the people applauding them weren't their parents and uncles and grannies. I quickly coax them back on for the encore—a stripped-down version of "Titanium", no David Guetta vibe, only Sia—and catch my mother looking at me and giving me a big thumbs-up.

✖ ✖ ✖

After the concert, there's a reception with freshly-pressed juices for the kids—my mother would never let them drink juice from a box—and wine for the adults.

"Now all you need is a girlfriend and you will have arrived," Clayton says. My brother always manages to inject some negativity into a great situation for me. He has done so from the moment I was born.

"Leave her alone, Clay," Dad says. "Let your sister enjoy this beautiful achievement."

I bask in my family's compliments—genuine and back-handed ones alike—for a while, until I crave the attention of my friends.

On my way over to where they're huddled together, I'm accosted by three parents—all of them single mothers—thanking me for making their kids sing. It truly is a glorious afternoon, because, and this I've only just recently come to learn, nothing compares to a child's unconditional admiration. When six-year-old Kelly rushed over to me after the final encore and threw her little arms around my neck, I felt it in every cell of my body. It was magic—and so much more emotionally fulfilling than the expectation-filled admiration of a woman looking to bed me after a solo gig.

"Have you all been moved to tears by my achievements?" I joke, when I arrive at my friends' table.

"Don't joke about that, Ali," Anna says, "I'm still a

blubbering mess."

Grace just opens her arms wide and gives me a hug. "Your job is so much more satisfying than mine."

Katherine just nods at me and doesn't say anything. She just stands there, glancing around awkwardly, as if the clock has been turned back a year and we've only just been re-introduced. Stubborn, grudge-holding Ali is starting to rear her head, and I'm of half a mind to just ignore her the way she's been ignoring me the past few weeks, but I just don't have it in me. Not today, after having been surrounded by the kids' pure elation at getting to do this, and spreading so much unadulterated joy.

"Did you enjoy it, Katherine?" I ask. She looks as though she'd rather shake my hand than exchange the peck on the cheek we've grown accustomed to. "Oh, that's right, you only caught the last song." I fix her with a stare that, I hope, expresses some of my disappointment.

"I'm so sorry, Ali. I had a work thing."

There she goes again with the work excuse. "Of course you did." I turn away from her, because I don't want her excuses and her disrespect for me to ruin more of my day. I feel it in the pit of my stomach nonetheless, this unexpected friendship we've built over the past months, crumbling just like that. But what more can I possibly do? I've contacted her over and over again only to be rejected every time. This ball's clearly no longer in my court.

"Ali," Katherine says from behind me. "I'm really sorry. Can we talk in private for a minute?"

I turn to face her. "*Now* you want to talk?" I give her a once-over. She looks a bit pale, like she hasn't been eating properly. "Well, you know what? Today, *I'm* busy."

I walk away from her because I'm starting to get really pissed off and I don't want the kids to see me that way.

CHAPTER TWENTY

KATHERINE

It's been two weeks since the MFTC concert. Two more weeks of extreme cowardice on my part and thus, two more weeks since I last saw Ali. Her ignoring me for the rest of the reception was definitely deserved, but it also made me realize that my feelings for her have not diminished one bit.

My plan is not working.

Thank goodness, I had to go to Chicago for work for the better part of the week, or I would have definitely cracked. Ali doesn't text me anymore to ask if I'll go to yoga. I haven't attended a single class since my epiphany, and I feel it everywhere. I don't sleep as well. I feel lifeless for most of the day. I need to drink double the amount of coffee I usually drink to keep me going in the afternoon. And all of that for what?

I sit in my bedroom, the vibrator Ali bought me the last time we really spoke in my hands. I haven't even taken it out of its box yet. I sit here and really ask myself why. What could be worse than this? Our friendship is already falling to pieces. I made a mistake. On top of that, I haven't just ignored Ali, I've ignored Grace and Anna as well, because I didn't want to subject myself to their scrutiny.

I need to get my life back. While I was trying not to act foolishly, I've accomplished the exact opposite. I'm on the cusp of forty and I'm sitting on the edge of my bed with a vibrator in my hands. This says a lot about my life, about what I've allowed it to turn into.

I grab my phone from the nightstand and call Grace. I tell her I've been stupid and a horrible friend and will she please meet me for coffee later.

"About fucking time, Katie," she says, and it sounds awkward because Grace is not someone who swears often. "Your timing is excellent though, because I have some pretty big news." She's such a tease.

We arrange to meet in a couple of hours and then I'm back to sitting on the bed with the vibrator. I open the box and take it out. It's a really fancy one, coated in smooth silver. Should I?

Why not?

I check the inside compartment for batteries, but it's empty. The box doesn't contain any either. My glance falls on the flashlight I keep on my nightstand for emergency situations. I grab it and screw the lid off. Yes. Exactly what I'm looking for. A good omen for the rest of the day, when I'll tell Grace about what's been bugging me.

I insert the flashlight's batteries into the vibrator and switch it on. The buzzing sound is something I haven't heard in a long time, but it sparks an immediate reaction between my legs. Suddenly, I feel like I really, really need this. Like I might explode if I don't bring this toy between my legs immediately.

I take off my jeans and panties and lie down on the bed with my legs spread wide. I lie still for a while, listening to my breath, enjoying the cool air between my legs. I begin to conjure up enticing images, flashes from movies I've seen, but, of course, Ali's face pops up immediately. There's no use fighting it. Not when I'm about to do this.

I switch the vibrator back on and rub it along my lips to warm it up a little, before letting it touch down on my most sensitive spot. The sensation is thrilling from the start, though I seem to remember from previous uses of similar toys that they vibrated more vigorously. Still, this should do the trick. Remain untouched long enough, and even the slightest vibration will do.

I unleash my subconscious and let it conjure up every image of Ali I've blocked over the past few weeks. Ali on stage, her hand in the air, just next to her cheek, passion visible even in her fingertips. That heavy-lidded look she has. Her chocolate-warm voice. That time I grabbed her hand. I'm so close, my muscles are already starting to tense. So close, my breath is starting to come out in bursts. Then the batteries die and I miss my climax. It peters out on me like the last drop drips out of a tap when you turn it off.

I laugh through my frustration because this is just so typical. So exemplary of what I've let my life become: an existence without joy, satisfaction always just out of reach.

No more, I tell myself. No more.

* * *

"Hey, stranger." Instead of hugging me, Grace thrusts her hand in my face. Her finger is decorated with a brand new ring.

My eyes widen. "No?" I ask.

"Oh, yes. Anna asked me to marry her last night. I said yes." Grace is jumping up and down with excitement.

"Oh my God, Gracie. Come here." I throw my arms around her and hug her for a long time.

"How about something stronger than coffee to celebrate?" she asks when we break from our hug.

"Excellent idea." Instead of entering the coffee house we stand outside of, we head to a bar across the street. Today, I have no objections to some daytime drinking. I'm so happy for Grace, though the thought does enter my mind that it's a bit soon. But, I guess, when you know, you know. Heck, even I knew from the first moment I saw the two of them together. Nothing has changed since then.

"Where have you been hiding? What's all this work nonsense you've been burying yourself in? I've missed you,"

Grace says. We've ordered a bottle of champagne, because what better occasion could there be? She pours me a glass and holds it up. "Tell me everything, but first, we toast!"

"To true love," I say, thinking of what I came here to tell her.

"To true love," Grace repeats, "and to what matters most, which is *not* work."

I deserve the admonishment, even though I haven't been working nearly as hard as Grace presumes. "I'm so happy for you and Anna." Maybe Anna is giving Ali the news as we speak.

"I'm over the moon." Grace's eyes are starting to glaze over already, though she's only had a few sips of champagne. It must be love, I conclude, making her look all mellow and utterly content.

Grace tells me all about how Anna proposed and how they were an emotional mess for the rest of the night and had to flee indoors to dry their tears.

"Of course," she says, after ending her tale, "we want our two best friends to be maids of honor." Her stare lingers on me. "So, whatever beef you've got going with Ali, it's time to grow up and get past it, Katie. I will not have tension at my wedding."

"About Ali…" I begin. "We don't have a beef. It's—it's silly."

"Good, then it will be easy to resolve, though you're going to have to take the initiative. I gather she's still upset about you as good as missing that concert. That was a really big deal to her. She really wanted us all there."

"I know. I screwed up." My stomach coils into a knot. "It's all my stupid, stupid fault."

"But what happened? All I know is that one moment you were getting along fine and the next you're not and we barely see you anymore. What's going on at work… or with you?"

I exhale a deep breath, then inhale deeply, trying to find

the courage. "During that blind date I went on with Greta…" I bury my face in my hands dramatically. Why is this so hard to say out loud? I look back up at Grace. "We ended up talking about Ali… a lot, and it made me see that, er, I wanted to be on a date with her rather than with Greta. I wanted to be more than just her friend."

Grace nods thoughtfully, her lips crunched together. "About time, Katie. For Christ's sake."

"What do you mean?" I'm so relieved I've just told someone, I don't get what she's saying.

"Let me tell you something Anna and I concluded that very first night we all met at that bar in Chelsea. At the time it might have been a silly thing to say, but when we went to dinner just the two of us after you ditched us, we predicted this. Well, I mean, not *this*." She gestures at me with her hand. "But that something would bloom between the two of you at some point. After you got over Susan. Because sometimes when you witness two people meeting, or seeing each other again after a long time, you can just tell. Even though you were still reeling from your break-up, and despite your history with Ali in college, we could sense that unquantifiable thing in the air between the two of you. So what you've just told me comes as no surprise."

I shake my head. "And to think I didn't want anyone to know. That's why I've been keeping my distance. I thought that if I just ignored her, and our mutual friends, it would just go away."

"Katie, come on, we've been friends forever. We're hardly *mutual* friends. I wish you would have come to me."

"I know. I wish I had too." I suddenly don't feel much like drinking champagne anymore, but I take a sip anyway. "How big is the damage I've done?"

"Ali is upset because, to her, it seems like you simply ditched her. For no good reason." Grace fiddles with her new ring.

"Do you think… er, she has any idea?"

"No. Why would she? We have talked about you and your disappearing act, but despite my suspicions, I would never say anything to anyone else without talking to you first. And you've been a bit hard to reach of late."

"That afternoon of the concert I wasn't really working. Just staring out of my window waiting for time to pass and, with every second that went by, I knew I was hurting her, and myself as well. Until I couldn't take it anymore and rushed uptown. It was so stupid."

"You're friends. Friendship doesn't get destroyed that fast. You have a solid foundation. I don't think Ali's one to hold a grudge, but... I think you have no other option than to tell her the truth."

"But... What if I tell her and, I don't know, she thinks I'm ridiculous for feeling the way that I do."

"Why on earth would she think that? You know Ali. In fact, you know her much better than I do. She wouldn't deliberately hurt you."

"Like I have done with her."

"You haven't deliberately hurt her." Grace grabs my hand. "You just didn't have a clue what to do."

"I don't know if I can face the rejection."

"Who says she's going to reject you?" Grace's expression is dead serious.

"Has she, er, said anything?"

"No, but, come on. You two have chemistry through the roof. I've known that for months now. I thought you were just biding your time, waiting for your heart to heal after Susan. That you didn't want Ali to be some sort of transitional person to get over Susan with."

"Honestly, until that date with Greta, I didn't have a clue what my true feelings were. But God, I've missed her so much the past few weeks. It's only when you stop seeing someone that you realize how much they mean to you."

"My best guess is that this might be one of the reasons Ali is so upset with you. I know for a fact that she misses you too. She told me."

"What should I do? Should I call her?"

Grace nods. "Yes. Call her right now. Set something up for as soon as possible."

Nerves tear through my belly. But I might as well do it with Grace—and a bottle of champagne—by my side. I take my phone and, without letting myself get caught up in contrary thoughts, dial her number. It rings a few times, then she picks up.

"Hello." Just hearing her voice is enough to have my breath catch in my throat.

"Ali, hi. It's me, Katherine," I stutter. "Erm, I was wondering if you'd like to meet up some time."

Silence on the other end of the line. When she doesn't say anything, I need to fill the silence.

"Are you free tonight by any chance?"

"No, Katherine." She's doing her best to make her voice sound formal. "I'm not free tonight."

"Do you have a gig?" I ask, hopeful. "I could come—"

"No, I have a date," she says matter-of-factly. Of course she has a date. Why wouldn't she? It's Saturday evening and she's Ali West.

"Oh, okay. Some other time?" I try to regroup but the adrenalin that rushed through me at the beginning of the call has made way for massive deflation. "Tomorrow maybe?"

"Yes, maybe in the evening." I can definitely hear the reluctance in Ali's voice. Perhaps she wants me to try harder.

"How about I cook you dinner?"

"Can I get back to you tomorrow? I'm not sure yet how my day will pan out."

"Yes, sure." I can only grovel.

"Okay. Bye." Without any further ceremony, she hangs up on me, and my heart drops all the way to the floor.

"She has a date tonight." Christ, I have difficulty keeping my tears at bay. What had I expected? That all I had to do was make a phone call and she'd come running into my arms?

"Come to ours. We'll watch Netflix and order pizza," Grace says.

I nod slowly. It's going to have to be one hell of a movie to keep my mind off Ali on her date.

ALI

Who does Katherine think she is? Does she really think she can call me and ask me if I'm free tonight, just like that? I know I'm probably overreacting, but her absence has affected me more than I thought it would. I've lost touch with friends before. Anna disappeared from my life for an entire year when she was shacking up with Grayson in New Jersey. It was just a case of our lives taking divergent paths. But with Katherine, it's different.

She works a block away from the studio where we used to take yoga every single week. That's how I know she's been actively avoiding me. And, for some reason, I didn't have it in me to just simply accept her invitation for tonight, or tomorrow, to listen to whatever crazy thing she'd have to say, and forgive her. She hurt me too much for me to give her that instant satisfaction. Even though I don't have plans at all tonight. No date, no gig.

When Katherine called, I was just on my way home from meeting Anna, who shared the news of her engagement to Grace with me. You'd think the love in Anna's gaze would have left me in a more forgiving mood, but it had the opposite effect.

Despite having just seen her in person, I call her.

"Katherine just called me." I cut to the chase. "She wanted to meet tonight, but I told her I couldn't because I have a date."

"Er, okay," Anna says. "Is it a hot date?"

"No, I don't actually have a date. I was just being stubborn."

"Why so stubborn?" Anna has a hint of glee in her voice I don't understand.

"Because why would I meet with her just because she calls? Why wouldn't I let her stew a little bit now that she has —I hope—finally realized she's been a really shitty friend."

"Ali, please. You're not a game player."

"I know. I'm not. But it looks like she made me into one."

"Try and patch things up with her, please?" Anna adopts a pleading tone. "She's Grace's best friend, so do it for me if not for yourself. I'm just appealing to your charitable side." She actually giggles.

"I don't understand what's so funny about this, Anna."

"Nothing, I swear to you. I'm just giddy with engagement bliss. I'm sorry things turned out the way they did between you and Katherine. But she's opening the door to you, Ali. Don't you at least want to know what happened?"

"Of course I do. But whether she tells me tonight or not, it will not erase the time I spent racking my brain, and actually questioning my own personality, as to what horrible thing I did to her to deserve that kind of behavior. She hurt me and she disrespected our friendship. I don't see how we could ever just go back."

"Because you *are* friends. These things happen all the time. Friendship isn't some perfect trajectory through life of sharing your dreams and hopes and aspirations and a few big moments with another person. Surely the time you and she have spent together counts for something, and at least for enough to take the time to listen to her. You don't know what she's going to say. Stop speculating. Hear her out. What's the worst that could happen? It can only make things better between the two of you than they are now."

"Getting engaged has certainly turned you into a fountain of wisdom."

"You know I'm right, Ali. Besides, I need you two to get along so you can help plan our wedding."

"I'm not making you any promises, Anna. You know I love you, but I have to draw the line somewhere."

"Just talk to her and see what happens."

"I will, but I'm not sure I want to tonight. Not just yet."

"Just follow your gut. You're good at that."

After we've hung up, I consider Anna's words. It certainly can't be worse between Katherine and me than it is now. I'm also really curious to find out what has been going on with her. Maybe she had some sort of melt-down she had to go through on her own. Because if I had offended her in some way, she would have told me. She always did in the past.

I consider texting her to accept her dinner invitation for tomorrow, but, before I do, I head to the Irish pub across the street from my building, for a much-needed late afternoon tipple.

★ ★ ★

Two hours later, I'm still at the bar. I got talking to Hilda, the bartender, who always has a good story to tell—and who mixes a mean Old Fashioned.

It's nearly seven when my phone beeps. It's a message from Anna, telling me that Katherine is coming over to theirs and asking me if I want to join.

Fuck, yeah, I type back, and that's how I know I'm drunk.

I order a double espresso and a glass of water from Hilda, then say my goodbyes to her and the rest of the regulars lining the bar with empty looks in their eyes. Outside, I flag down a cab with a shaky arm, and head to Grace and Anna's place. This should be a fun night. So much better than going on a date.

I arrive at the same time as the pizza delivery guy. I pay him and tip him handsomely, then ring the bell.

"Delivery," I shout when the door is opened. I hold the boxes in front of my face so I don't see until I lower them that it's actually Katherine opening the door for me.

"Ali." Obviously, she doesn't know what to think. As far as she knows, I'm on a date.

"Hey," I reply, remaining motionless in the door frame.

Grace comes over and takes the pizza boxes from me. The cab ride has sobered me up a bit, and the smell of pizza is making me very hungry.

"You guys talk. I'll keep these warm." Grace taps the boxes. "Go in the other room." She points at their guest room.

Katherine stands around looking as though she still needs to process my out-of-the-blue arrival.

"Do you want to talk?" I ask, my voice coming out much more gentle than I had planned.

Katherine nods and walks to the guest room. She sits down in the only armchair, so I take a seat on the bed. She looks pale like a sheet. Oh God. She's not sick, is she? "Are you okay?" Concern muscles its way to the front of my brain, through my receding tipsiness.

"I'm fine, Ali, I just—I'm sorry. I, er, I don't know how —" She falls silent.

"I know I told you I was going on a date, but I lied. It was stupid. I just wanted to spite you. Anna just texted me that you were here and I came straight over. I don't want to play games with you." I look at her quivering lips and her tapping foot. "But you have me worried now. What's going on?"

She shakes her head. "This is not the time and place I wanted to tell you this. It's not right, but…"

"Tell me what, Katherine?" I urge. I've waited weeks to find out.

"I—" She looks me in the eyes briefly, then glances

back to whatever fascinating thing her hands are doing in her lap. "I can't stop thinking about you. I might well be in love with you. I certainly have feelings for you, and I don't really know what to do about that," she blurts out.

My jaw drops. Did I hear that right? Because her delivery of the words didn't exactly match their meaning. Katherine Shepherd has feelings for me? "That's why you've been ignoring me for more than a month?"

"What else was I going to do?"

"Er, tell me about it. We're friends, remember?"

"I just wanted you to know. I'm deeply sorry for the way I behaved. It was stupid, childish even. I just didn't want to lose you and I honestly didn't know where my head was at. Nor do I know what to do about these feelings."

Then her words really register. This isn't about salvaging what's left of our friendship anymore. This isn't about apologies and choosing to accept them or not. This is about Katherine and me being much more than friends. "Wow, I… I don't really know what to say."

"You don't have to say anything." She does look at me now. "This is *my* problem."

"I'm just a little shocked, you know?" I rise from the bed. "I need to do some processing."

"I just wanted you to know. I don't expect anything from you. I know very well that we're just friends, and I hope we can some day magically go back to our old selves. Just know that I'm not avoiding you because of something you said or did. It's just me and my… silly feelings."

"Your feelings are not silly." I don't think I've ever been more flattered by someone confessing their infatuation with me. But how can I play this out without hurting her? I can't just look her in the eyes and tell her I feel the same. This is too much of a surprise for me to so quickly come to that conclusion. I also don't want to leave her hanging. God, I fully understand why she avoided me. This situation is impossible.

"I think I'm just going to go home. It would be awkward for me to stay." Her voice is a mere whisper.

"I'll go, if it makes you more comfortable." I need to stop myself from grabbing her hand. It's not as though I've never considered the possibility… of us doing things. But having that kind of relationship with each other? This is something I will need some time to seriously consider, lest more feelings get hurt.

"I've just made a massive fool of myself, so it really doesn't matter anymore at this point whether I'm comfortable or not," she says.

"No, please don't think that. I just need some time. I don't think that's too much to ask."

"It's not. I just… miss us. I miss what we had. I miss hanging out with you. Standing here now, after having just said this, I know it will never be the same again. I could blame myself for not handling it better, but the thing is that I have no idea how I could have done that. This is just one of life's cruel pranks. I…" She pauses, takes a breath. "I'm in love with you, Ali. It's as simple as that. It has taken a lot for me to get to this point and be able to admit that, first to myself, then to Grace, and now to you. There's nothing more I can say." She takes a step towards the door. "You take all the time you need."

"Katherine." I try to stop her from leaving, but she's out of the room before I can say more.

When I'm in the living room, I just see her gather her things, mumble a few words to Anna and Grace, and leave.

Shit.

Katherine's in love with me.

CHAPTER TWENTY-ONE

KATHERINE

To my surprise, on Sunday morning, I wake up from a refreshingly good night's sleep. It must have been the relief of unburdening myself. Living with a secret will keep you up at night. Though I do feel as though my fate rests entirely in Ali's hands now. What did she do after I fled Grace and Anna's? I couldn't possibly stay. I had exposed myself too much for that. It was a little immature to run out on Ali like that, but I needed some time to get my bearings. To return to myself after stepping so far out of my comfort zone.

Apparently, I'm a woman who'd rather let a friendship wither and die instead of telling her friend that she has feelings for her. If there's some sort of gut instinct that comes with falling in love and making the right moves when you do, I don't think I have it. I'm sure I don't have it, in fact, what with the way I acted.

But now, here I sit, refreshed, a little less mortified, but on pins and needles nonetheless. I can only wait. Or no, I can call Grace. And ask her if Ali has said anything. Ideally, all of this would have unfolded privately between Ali and me, and not in our friends' guest room, but, then again, it was Grace who made me call Ali in the first place. Both Grace and Anna have their noses deep inside our private business, so I might as well make use of that fact. Anything is better than sitting here and waiting. And it's Sunday. Even

I don't go into the office on a Sunday.

I call Grace and ask her flat-out what Ali said after I left.

"She was, er, how to say this… surprisingly flabbergasted," Grace says. "Turns out she didn't have a clue."

"I don't think that's so surprising." Just talking to Grace, and remembering the minutiae of last night, makes my stomach tense. "How could she possibly have guessed?"

"Female intuition. I've always thought Ali to be a very intuitive person."

"Well, maybe she just didn't want to go there. Maybe it's just too inconceivable. We're so different."

"*You* went there," Grace says. "That's proof enough that anything is possible."

"Did she say anything that I should know about?"

"No," Grace pauses, presumably to think. "She didn't say much at all. She looked mostly stunned. Had a slice of pizza and then left. To process the news, I guess."

"I don't know what I'm supposed to do now. Just wait? Because that's driving me crazy."

"She'll be in touch soon enough. I'm pretty sure of that."

"It feels like waiting for exam results. Like everything is out of my hands now."

"Remember what you were like in college and what I used to say to you? Calm down, Pussycat, you've done all you can and you know you've done well." She follows up with a chuckle.

"This situation is very different. Having done my best won't influence the outcome here."

"I know this is stressful, Katie, but hang in there. And keep me posted. You can call me anytime."

We hang up and I'm no wiser than before I called Grace. I'll be damned if I'm just going to sit around and wait for my phone to ring. I'm going for a walk, perhaps stop at the farmers' market. Do ordinary Sunday activities.

★ ★ ★

I've just bought a pound of apples, when my phone rings. I balance my shopping bag in one hand while frantically searching for the thing in my bag. I look at the screen and my heart skips a beat. It's her.

"Hello." My voice is shaky.

"Hey, er, it's me." I always find it so stupid when people say that, but I'm guilty of doing it myself and when Ali says it, it's just so damn cute.

"Hey." As far as phone conversations go, this one is starting off pretty high on the scale of awkwardness. I move away from the stalls and find a spot where I can talk more privately. I would like to have been home for this particular conversation.

"I didn't sleep much last night," she says.

"Oh." My heart flings itself against my ribcage with escalating force. *Just tell me*, I think. As though this is even a possibility. There are so many outcomes here. So many ways in which I can get hurt. But at least I've been honest.

"We need to talk about this, Katherine."

"Yeah." I've been reduced to monosyllabic words. The ridiculous pounding of my heart must be sucking away all the blood from my brain.

"How about we go on a date?" Ali asks, her voice all sultry in my ear. I nearly drop my apples.

"Er, yes, I would like that very much." Thank goodness I haven't lost my ability to speak full sentences.

"A proper date," she says, "not just two friends having a meal." She pauses. "Just to see what it feels like."

"Okay," I say greedily.

We arrange a time and place and when we hang up, my hand trembles more than my voice did when I picked up. I'm going on a date with Ali.

The first thing I do is look for the earliest yoga class this afternoon so I can calm myself down before meeting her.

ALI

Katherine has dressed casually for our date. I told her once that I like how different she looks in just jeans and a blouse. She must have remembered. It strips away a layer of formality and makes her come across more accessible and relaxed.

We kiss each other on the cheek and it feels awkward and sweet at the same time. When she sits down across from me I can immediately tell she's nervous. Her glance skitters from here to there. She fiddles with her phone, puts it away, takes it out of her bag again. Katherine is not cut out for this. For this not knowing what will happen. I don't know what's going to happen either.

When you become close friends with someone, especially a fellow lesbian, there comes a time when you just cross over into the platonic-only zone, and you start seeing the person differently. More like family than a potential love interest. That's how I've regarded Katherine for a while now, although, as I was tossing and turning through the night, I had to—very freely—admit that, between her and me, there's always been this undercurrent of possibility. But because of the circumstances under which we became reacquainted, I easily shoved that initial spark to the side, because she was such an emotional wreck back then, and then I just made a habit of continuing to do so.

"I think I'll have the grilled radicchio," she says.

"Look, Katherine." I try to smile reassuringly. "When I asked you out, I really asked you out." If I want her to enjoy this night at all, I'm going to have to find a way to unwind her uptightness a little. "I hope you can tell the difference." What I would really like to do is grab her hand, rub my thumb on her palm, and reassure her in a different way. This is nerve-racking for me, too. And that's what I would usually do. "Take a deep breath."

"I went to a yoga class this afternoon," she says. "But all it did was remind me of you. I could never fully relax."

"Let's both take a breath and start again." I cock my head. "You look really nice tonight, by the way."

"I'm so nervous. This is so… difficult. I'm afraid to say or do the wrong thing, which is ridiculous, because you already know me so well, and I know that it probably doesn't make that much difference if I make a fool of myself again tonight, but I just can't shake the feeling that I'm taking a test or something."

"Take that breath," I urge. "Then we'll order a bottle of wine."

She inhales deeply, her glance moving to and fro. I breathe with her. Because how do we do this? How do we go from friends to lovers? It's not a matter of me not being attracted to her. I've always thought her smoking hot and if she were to get up, take my hand, and say, "Have your way with me, Ali," I would be up for that, but I'd still be left with the same question afterwards. Do we belong together? The only way to know for sure, is to try. But I do have the expectation on me that comes with Katherine's love declaration. At the core of it, we are friends first. This is a brand new situation for me too.

We order food and copious drinks and are then left staring into each other's eyes again. When I look into Katherine's blue eyes, it's not hard to see how we could be happy together. We've already established that, against all odds, we get along. I've always wanted to find out what it would be like to sleep with her. However, this is all still supposition and I won't know anything for sure until it's real.

"We've come a long way since college," I say, to re-break the ice. It keeps forming between us, as though the temperature in this restaurant—or perhaps just around our table—keeps plummeting.

The fact of the matter is that I've never entered a relationship with anyone before testing our sexual chemistry first. It was never a conscious strategy, but that's just the way it has always been. What we're trying to do now, is the complete opposite of what I'm used to.

"We've changed a lot," Katherine says. "We'll always be very different people, but I think our personalities have mellowed and, perhaps, gravitated toward each other. We have more middle ground to find ourselves on. It started with just a sliver, and look at me now." She finally manages a smile. Is this Katherine in seduction mode? She's driving me a little crazy already. "Now I want it all," she adds.

"When you yelled at me outside the library all those years ago, I wanted you a little already."

"I don't believe that for a second. You despised the hell out of me. And I had just blackmailed your lover."

"So what? All of that doesn't mean that I didn't want you a little." I do put my hand on hers now. She flinches for a split second, more because of shock than anything else, I hope, but doesn't retract.

"You wanted *everyone* back then."

"That's absolutely not true." My thumb slips underneath her hand, finding her palm. "I have standards. Anyway, let's not talk about the past. Let's talk about the present."

She sinks her teeth into her bottom lip and, like I did once before, I get an inkling of what she would be like in bed. I predict that it's the one spot where she lets go of all her inhibitions. Now that I've made up my mind about that, I'm going there. I want her. I'm all in. It's the only way I know.

"You mean let's flirt some more?"

"I'm going to be honest with you. I didn't know you had it in you. When you walked in here, you looked so scared, I thought you might just walk out again. But look at you now." I lower my voice. "You're turning me on."

Her lips widen into a slow smile. "I've got game," she says, and that suddenly sounds so ridiculous, we both break out into a chuckle.

"Of course you do," I say after we catch our breath and I mean it.

"Thank you for asking me out." She sounds confident now, as a woman who knows exactly what she wants.

"What else was I going to do? Ignore you for weeks on end?" I can't help playing with her a little.

She shakes her head. "It was pure torture, Ali, trust me. I missed you like crazy."

"I missed you too."

When a waiter comes over, I let go of Katherine's hand. We eat and drink and flirt some more, until I can't take it anymore, and ask for the check.

"Where to now?" I ask, when we're shuffling our weight around on the sidewalk. Our date has reached the next level, and there's another gate of awkwardness to pass through. If it were any other woman, by now, after the level of flirting we've already engaged in, I wouldn't even ask. I would just flag down a cab and head over to my place. But tonight, everything is different.

"Nightcap?" she asks.

"Yes, please." I finally grab her hand again. It already feels so comfortable in mine, as if it belongs there.

"Let's go to yours."

And we do.

CHAPTER TWENTY-TWO

KATHERINE

When we arrive at Ali's apartment, I want her to take me by the hand once again, and lead me straight to her bedroom, but I also don't want her to do that. The entire evening has been a rollercoaster of emotions and Ali is not someone I can just jump into bed with. With her, it needs to be more than dinner and a cab ride home. Because she has probably done this a million times before, usually even skipping the dinner part, and I want to be more to her. I'm also scared of how she would feel in the morning. What if this experience turns out to be no different to her than all her previous ones? It might ruin everything.

I do vow that, before the night is over and I return home—because that's another vow I make—I will kiss her. I have dreamed of her lips on mine one too many times to resist that. The way things have been going, I think a kiss is definitely on the cards.

"Bourbon?" she asks, already heading to the liquor cabinet.

I shake my head. "I don't want a headache in the morning."

"Coffee? Tea?" She leans against the wall, her ankles crossed, her neck slanted, with her gaze on me the way I've seen it land on a dozen other women before me, and an arrow of lust burrows straight through me.

"Just you," I say, surprising myself most of all. Oh shit, there goes my vow. What am I doing? I'm not reckless. I'm cautious. "Or some water," I quickly add.

"You can have both." She doesn't turn around immediately, but stands there pinning her glance on me a while longer. She's dressed in her usual palette of yellows and browns and, courtesy of the locker rooms we've shared, I've seen what she looks like underneath.

At this moment, Ali isn't my friend anymore. I might as well just have met her tonight and been seized by extreme infatuation, mingled with supreme lust and the desire to tear those clothes off her. My mind shifts from seeing her as the woman who was there for me after Susan dumped me, to the woman she must be to many others. Highly seductive, skilled at flirtation, tons of experience in bed. And I want the Ali West experience, but not like anyone else has had it before. I want it forever. Because a lust like this is foreign to me, and I know full well I wouldn't be standing here, on wobbly knees in her living room, wanting her so badly I'm about to forget my own name, if I didn't know her through and through. If I didn't know the human being underneath.

When she does finally head into the kitchen to fetch some water, I find myself following her, like I can't be away from her. That's when I realize I won't be going home tonight. The attraction is too great. I wouldn't be able to tear myself away from her. I feel as though she has already kissed me a thousand times. I feel so ready, despite my resolutions, and perhaps it's only logical, because I don't need to get to know her any better.

"Hey," she says when I turn up in the kitchen. "That thirsty, huh?"

I just nod, then I lunge for her. I wrap my hands around her neck and pull her to me, look into her eyes for the briefest of instants, before pressing my lips to hers. I can't wait. I've waited forever. I've waited for my heart to heal, and it has, and now it's ready for her.

When our lips meet, an exquisite dizziness takes hold of me, as though I'm thrown into a spiral of extreme sensitivity and forwardness and letting go. Because I've wanted to kiss her for a while now. I've wanted to since long before I knew I did. Long before I told her. Long before this moment, when our lips finally meet.

She wraps her arms around my waist and pulls me even closer. When our lips part to catch our breath, the smile she shoots me is so heart-warming, so obvious in all it wants to convey, that I instantly reach for her again, and kiss her as though she is the first and last person I've ever kissed and will. And I don't know when the paths of our lives started to converge in the way they did to bring us together. Maybe everything that has happened up until now has been a detour, a means to make us evolve in the right direction and prepare us for this. For the inevitable, because that's how this kiss feels: inevitable. Meant to be.

"Do you want that water?" she asks when we break again. My lips already feel numb because of too much sensation, too much Ali. Maybe I should take a step back here and let her take the lead, because that's how I always believed it would be. I never thought I'd pounce on her the way I did, when I finally got permission to. I never even dared to dream of this moment. This moment when all my dreams are coming true. That's what baffles me most of all. Right now, I'm unafraid. I'm so caught up in lust's hold that I don't care what happens next, and that I have faith that it will be good, that it can't be anything else, because just standing here with her already feels so good.

"Fuck no," I say to her smiling face. "I only want you."

A serious expression crosses her face. Is this where I overstep? Move too soon, because, after all, I'm the one who came forward with my feelings and piled a bunch of expectations on her? In no way did I leave my house tonight expecting this. What's happening right now, and what I hope is yet to come, is by no means a given. We are two individuals, and while I have made my intentions very clear, I've yet to hear a word about that from Ali. Though her body language has already told me plenty—all I need to know. Or I wouldn't still be here.

ALI

"Let's talk for a second." I don't move away from Katherine, because I don't want to give her the wrong impression, but I need this to be right, to not be this frenzy we're about to launch ourselves into.

She nods, and I don't detect any immediate disappointment on her face. A kiss is one thing, but what comes next, though there's not a flicker of doubt in my mind that I want it, is something else. A kiss we could bounce back from, but if we mess up the next part, we could cause irreparable damage. It's not like me to be so thoughtful. I'm used to trusting my instincts one hundred percent, but some women—perhaps only one—deserve my thoughtfulness because of what they mean to me.

I pour us both a glass of water and when I hand it to her, and our fingers touch, we both stare at them as though wanting to examine the cause of the fireworks exploding throughout our flesh—at least that's what it feels like for me.

"Katherine." I take a quick sip and put my glass on the kitchen counter—we keep having these kinds of talks in odd places. "I can't stand here and tell you in good faith that I feel exactly the same about you as how you described the way you feel about me. On this road we're now on together, I think you might be a few lengths ahead of me. This doesn't mean that I can't, and do not desperately want to catch up, but I'm just not there yet. What I do know, though, is what I feel in here." I take her hand and bring it to my chest, laying it over my heart. "It's messy in there, I won't lie. But I already love you as my friend and I want more. I'm not saying that friendship plus sleeping together will and can automatically equal a relationship, but I sure do want to try."

She looks at our hands over my chest, then back up to my face. "Then let's try." She puts her water glass away and steps closer, looking deep into my eyes. "I appreciate your honesty." She brings a finger to my cheek and gently caresses me, and I melt inside. If this is the effect a simple touch has on me, I'm sure I'll catch up to her quickly.

I grab her hand again and bring it to my mouth, and kiss all five of her knuckles. Then I want her so badly, I don't want to talk anymore. I just want to be—really be—with her.

"Come on." I lead her to my bedroom, where my bed is unmade as usual. The room is messy, but cozy, and it doesn't even matter. A year ago I would have wondered what Katherine thought of a grown-up sleeping in an untidy room like this, but now, I don't wonder anything. Or no, that's a lie. I wonder how her skin will yield to my touch, how her muscles will contract when she comes, how my fingers on her will make her scream out. I don't know how or why, but I just know she'll be a screamer. She keeps too much inside in her day-to-day life to not be one.

I stand in front of her and smile. Just that smile alone feels like enough. Though that's probably because what's coming next is inevitable. Written in the stars. Perhaps it always was.

I pull her to me, gentler this time, and when our lips part and our tongues mingle, I commit her taste to memory. Her hands are on my back, her fingers applying the mildest of pressure. She's not rushing. She's allowing me to catch up.

I've barely seen her naked because when we're in the locker room she's always doing this ridiculous dance with her towel, as though what she's hiding under there is top secret and we don't all have the same parts. So now I'm in a hurry to tug her blouse over her head, but I owe it to this moment to take my time. This can't be anything less than perfect.

This new beginning for us. I want us to start off on the right foot. So, instead, I slowly start unbuttoning her blouse, taking my time with each button, in between our lips and tongues meeting, until the front of it is open and I just have to look. I take a small step back and part the sides of her blouse.

Blood rushes between my legs as I watch her standing there. She's like a new person. This woman has nothing to do with the girl I met in college. She is beautiful and, despite putting her heart on the line, she oozes a sexy sort of confidence that I just want to lap up.

With her hands, she shifts the blouse off her and lets it drop to the carpet. She's in jeans and just her bra now and it's an image I want to etch in my memory forever.

Next, she comes for me. She grabs the hem of my top and pulls it over my head.

"I want you," Katherine says, and her words echo back from every cell of my body.

CHAPTER TWENTY-THREE

KATHERINE

My flesh feels like it might explode, as though just stripping Ali of her top is already too much. But I want so much more. It's a miracle that I'm standing here in her bedroom, but, on the other hand, it also feels like we've finally reached a conclusion. In this moment, I don't care that her feelings are not exactly the same as mine, all I care about is that we're here together, and I'm more than ready for what's about to happen next.

She gropes for my jeans button first and flips it open while she runs her lips over my neck, up to my mouth again, and then pulls me close to her by the waistband.

"I want you too," she says, and in my foolish, foolish head, it already sounds like "I love you".

Ali abandons my jeans and brings her hands to my back, where they unclasp my bra. I unglue myself from her for an instant to let it fall over my arms, through the gap between our bodies, where it joins my blouse on the carpet. I'm not shy to stand in front of her like this. Not now. The air on my nipples has an instant effect, and, oh, I want to see her, too. I mimic exactly what she just did to me, and then we're both naked from the waist up.

Seeing her like this while her eyes are on me, catapults me to the next level, and now it's my turn to grab for her pants button. I want them off. I want her naked.

I start pushing her pants off her, and she helps me by wiggling her ass and soon she's kicking them off her feet. Her panties are cream colored and create an effect so gorgeous with her dark skin, I just want to stare at them for an instant. But Ali comes for me next and before I know it I'm standing in front of her in only my panties as well.

When I look into her eyes, I can see her impatience grow in them. She kisses me again, but with more insistence this time, and starts walking me backwards to the bed.

When the backs of my knees touch the mattress, I lose my balance and crash down onto it. I look up at her, at how she towers over me, her beautiful breasts right in front of my eyes. I feel myself go wet like a river.

She plants her knees on either side of me, straddling me, and throws her arms around my neck. The silk of her panties slides across my thighs and I know I'm close to the moment when something inside of me is about to unleash. The moment where the pressure gets too big and my body will take over. When I'm no longer Katherine Shepherd, CFO of Powell & Cooper, lousy friend at times. All that's left of me is the woman about to surrender to Ali.

She pushes me down onto the bed and I crawl backwards until my entire body is supported. She showers me in kisses, her knee burrowing between my legs, her skin everywhere on mine.

Her lips are on my neck, my jaw, my cheeks. She's everywhere and I'm starting to melt under her touch. She pushes herself away from me for an instant, looks into my eyes, cracking the tiniest of smiles, and I want to say it, want to say those two words that always turn me on so much, but I don't know if I can just yet.

She stares down at me, then bends over and traces a moist path with her lips to my breasts. She takes one of my nipples into her mouth and sucks on it gently, then repeats the process with the other.

Then, I can't hold it in any longer. I grab her by the

back of the head, pull her towards me, and whisper in her ear, "Fuck me." In my head, all I hear is echoes of "Fuck me, Ali. Fuck me."

My panties are burning a hole in my skin; they're too much, I want them off me and I want her inside.

In response, Ali glances at me again—no sign of a smile this time. She looks deep into my eyes, as though searching for a message in them, but I believe I've already made my intentions clear. Then her eyes go a little darker, and I know—I just do—that she's about to do what I just asked of her.

"Ask me again," she says, her voice low and breathy.

"Fuck me." Saying the words out loud again unleashes another flood between my legs. I'm so wet for her, so easy.

We've had a lifetime of foreplay.

She gives the slightest, almost imperceptible nod. Then she brings a hand to my cheek and, with one finger, draws a line over my skin all the way to my bellybutton. I break out into goose bumps and my impatient muscles make me squirm underneath her touch. She circles her fingertip around my bellybutton, then takes it down and hooks it underneath the waistband of my soaked panties. She just lets it lie there for a second, while she looks into my eyes again. Does she want me to say it again? Or is my desire clear in my glance?

Her finger delves deeper, surely encountering some of my extreme wetness. Her eyes stay glued to mine. With one hand, she starts tugging my panties down. I'm happy to lend a hand, and I have them off me in no time.

Then there I lie. Naked in front of Ali West. Ready for the taking. My clit pulses wildly, my nipples are so hard I'm painfully aware of them.

"Please," I hear myself beg, though I'm hardly the begging kind.

Ali licks her lips, then brings them down to me again and while she kisses me deeply, her finger skates along my drenched lips down there.

As soon as her finger touches down, she pushes herself up again and looks at me, as though she's amazed by what she's just found. By my immense arousal for her.

She narrows her eyes, and I spread my legs wider. She has a fingertip at my entrance. My whole body pulses with the need to feel it inside.

I'm about to beg her again, but I don't have to, because then she slips her finger inside. She does so ever so slowly, and every millimeter of ground she gains is magnified throughout my entire body. I feel her entering me in every cell, every extremity. She's still taking her sweet time, going excruciatingly slowly, as though wanting to discover me at a dignified pace. Her eyes are still on me as she pulls back out, even slower than her first stroke inside of me, and then she repeats the process. She's taking her time as if this first intimate encounter deserves the maximum amount of respect. No matter what she's trying to accomplish—tease me, respect me, or just plain turn me on beyond belief—it's working, because every time her finger touches down deep inside of me, it connects with a long-forgotten part of me.

"What are you doing?" I hear myself stutter as I look into her dark, dark eyes, my nails digging deep in the skin of her arm.

Her reply is another slow stroke, and this time, at the deepest point, I start to lose myself a little more. My entire body is clasping itself around Ali's one finger, like it never wants to let go of it again.

Then she starts increasing the pace—in her eyes, I can see she's starting to lose herself a little as well—and her strokes turn into thrusts, and then she's really having me, claiming me, even though I've been hers for a long time already.

I start to fall apart under her gaze, under her thrusts, my flesh igniting under her touch. This moment is the culmination of all the encounters we've had on the road that has led us here. When my skin starts to break out into tiny explosions and my muscles succumb to skin-deep earthquakes, I come for this moment that we're sharing, but also for all the ones that have come before and have brought us here.

"Oh, Ali," I gasp. I jut my hips forward, to catch and enhance the effect of every last one of her strokes. The tingle spreads though me, travels under my skin, explodes in my belly. I relax my neck muscles so that when the climax seizes me, my head is thrown back into the pillow, and I'm not looking into her eyes. But I see them anyway. They're projected on the back of my eyelids, guiding me, spurring me on. My inner walls grip Ali's finger tightly—is it still only the one? It's impossible to tell. All I know is that Ali just made me come and I'm in seventh heaven.

ALI

I let Katherine regroup a little. My insides are on fire. Watching her climax made me go weak at the knees. Because that was an entirely different Katherine Shepherd looking back at me. She didn't even avert her gaze until the very last moment.

I bring the finger I fucked her with to my mouth and lick her juices off it—a whole new way of getting acquainted with her.

Once she's caught her breath, she pulls me on top of her, and says, "Holy fuck." On my left arm, I can feel where her nails left marks. I slip myself on top of her entirely, my thigh lodging itself between her legs for an instant, and coming away all wet. It's quite something to have experienced Katherine's arousal for me. To have witnessed her surrender herself to me. On that road I spoke to her about earlier, I've gained some ground. And I don't need to wait until tomorrow morning to know how I'm going to feel about tonight. The realization is already hitting me from all sides. I feel it when I look into her eyes, when our skin meets, when, like now, she's slowly starting to push me off her. I want her just as badly.

This is the opposite of a one-night stand.

Katherine slides out from under me and, when she flanks me, has a huge grin on her face.

"What?" I ask, while her hand finds mine and she interlaces her fingers through mine.

"Nothing." She shakes her head. "I just… haven't felt this happy in a very long time."

"Imagine if you'd told me sooner," I joke. "All that time we wasted. We could have been engaged by now, like Grace and Anna."

She chuckles, then her expression goes serious again. "No talk of engagements just yet. I haven't even tasted you." With that, she crawls on top of me and starts kissing me. It begins at my earlobe and then suddenly her hands and her lips are everywhere. Fingers pinch my nipples. Her tongue is in my bellybutton. Her lips plant a kiss just above the waistband of my panties.

"You are so beautiful," she says, just before she tugs my panties down. I never had any issue believing anyone who spoke those words to me, but when Katherine says them they mean something else. Something deeper. It's not flattery. It's a statement coming from the bottom of her heart.

Then, her face disappears between my legs. My knees have fallen wide and I feel her breath on me. Her lips are on my inner thigh, inching upwards. Oh Christ, Katherine Shepherd is about to go down on me. Glimpses of memories flash through my mind. That time at Temptation when I flirted with her. The Powell & Cooper Christmas party. All the times things could have gone differently between us. Yet, it doesn't matter because here we are now.

And there's her tongue, connecting with my clit. Instantly, my muscles freeze. It feels so different when she licks me there. Of course, every woman is different, but when you've lived the life I've lived, at times, a tongue is more a means to an end than anything else. But not tonight. Not when Katherine's tongue connects with my flesh and the slightest flick of it reverberates throughout my entire being. As I lie here, my breath catching in my throat already, I know this is the kind of event I will have to write a song about. The emotion is so strong, it will need to burrow its way out of my soul at some point, to relive it, over and over again.

While there have been times I thought about Katherine and me between the sheets, somehow, an image of what she's doing right now never made it to the forefront of my mind. Looking at her, I'd envisioned a pillow princess, giving instructions, but not this. Not her unleashing the power of her tongue on my wet, wet pussy lips. I know it's a silly thought, but not surprising as our entire history is made up of assumptions about each other—wrong and right.

Her tongue slides between my lips now, up and down, always giving my clit a slight nudge on the up. She's starting to drive me crazy, and isn't that the strangest thing of all? Memories keep flooding my brain as I lose more control. Her sneaking into the back of the room at the MFTC concert. Her eyes on me when I'm doing a gig. Her admonishing tone when Mia hit on me at the Christmas party. The sadness in her eyes when Anna and Grace introduced us to each other. It all blends into one, then crystalizes into the image of her surrendering to my touch earlier, when she threw her head back into the pillows, and just forgot about where she was for an instant. When my touch did that to her.

She's focusing on my clit again, lavishing it with quick flicks of her tongue, alternated with long, luxurious licks. I dig my fingertips into her scalp. I glance down for an instant, and see her blonde hair contrasting with my dark skin. I see her head move with what she's doing to me. The sight is intoxicating. But what is truly arousing is that she's bringing a few fingers into play now. I feel their pressure along the rim of my pussy. She pushes them in high and deep—without mercy—while sucking my clit into her mouth fully and oh—

I fall down the depths of my desire, of the years we might have missed, and the fact that we've finally made it here. We're together, and the thought sneaks up on me that the reason why I never settled down with anyone before is because I was waiting for someone like her. Someone to take their time to get to know me. A friend turned lover. Perhaps, for me, it was the only way.

The orgasm shoots through me, its warmth spreading from my core to my limbs, and I let go of her head, let myself crash onto the bed, because I've surrendered to her as well.

When Katherine emerges from between my legs, her lips all glossy and sticky, a burst of happiness erupts within me. And I know. I might not have been able to see it until she told me, but I see now. She's the one that I've been waiting for—despite the fact that I've never felt as though I was waiting for anyone to complete my life.

Coyly, she sinks her teeth into her bottom lip.

"Come here." I pull her towards me. "That was pretty spectacular." I kiss her on the cheek.

"Yeah? Would you like me to do that again some time?"

"Not before I do it to you first." I look up at her, at the sparkle in her eyes.

"I guess I'll have to stay over then." She leans in and kisses me and I can smell myself all over her.

CHAPTER TWENTY-FOUR

KATHERINE

The first thing that enters my mind as I open my eyes is work. I conveniently managed to forget about it last night, what with my head—and other body parts—being so full of all things Ali.

I push myself up, looking around for an alarm clock. Light already slants through the blinds. While I glance around the room, my gaze falls on Ali, and I calm down. What a night we had. I couldn't have imagined it any better. I can't help myself, I lean over and kiss her on the cheek. Part of me wants to wake her up. Wants to share this supreme joy with her.

From the corner of my eye, while my lips land on her cheek over and over again, the smell of sex penetrating my nose, I see that it's 7 a.m. Despite a very late night, my internal clock hasn't let me down.

"Morning," Ali groans when she opens her eyes.

Instantly, I melt again. I want to pour my body all over hers. I want to taste her all over again. I want to scrub her skin clean in the shower and then coat it with my juices again. Most of all, I don't want to leave this bed.

"It's Monday," I say matter-of-factly. "I should get ready for work."

"Do you need to borrow a pair of panties?" Her eyes smile along with her lips.

"Or I could call in sick. Tell them I'm suffering from an acute case of infatuation."

Ali widens her eyes. "You? Call in sick? Is it the apocalypse?"

It is in my heart, I want to say, but that sounds way too corny. "I'm owed months of untaken leave. They can give me a day to recover from this." My hand is already crawling up her belly.

"From what, Katherine?" Ali catches my hand with hers, stops it in its tracks. Despite having known her for so long, and having just spent the night with her, I feel as though I've only scratched the surface of Ali West.

"Multiple orgasms and the effect of them on my brain. I might have lost my ability to count." I wrestle my hand free from her grip. "It would be downright irresponsible of me to work on next year's budget today. I'd get all the numbers wrong."

"If you call in sick, I will do the same." She grabs my hand again and brings it to her mouth, plants a kiss on my palm. "I need to find out what else these can do." She kisses my fingertips.

"Deal." I slide on top of her and kiss her on the mouth, my desire flaring up instantly. This will be a Monday well spent.

Without a twinge of guilt, I call the office and tell them I'm feeling unwell.

✶ ✶ ✶

Ali has made me pancakes just like the first time I stayed over. This time, we eat them naked from the waist up and feed each other pieces dripping with maple syrup.

"Not too much of a sugar bomb?" she asks, after swallowing the last bite.

"I think I burned off enough calories last night." I can't stop grinning.

"When did you know?" she asks.

She doesn't need to say anything more for me to

understand what she's getting at. "When you set me up with Greta." I can't keep my eyes off her lips, the hollow of her neck, her breasts. "All we ended up doing was talk about you. I guess I was disappointed I was sitting across from her, not you. Then it just hit me. Like a realization that had been lying in wait forever."

"Poor Greta." Ali pours us some more coffee. "She really liked you."

"I'm sorry but, you know, the heart wants what the heart wants." I catch her foot between my ankles.

"One thing's for sure, my parents will be over the moon and my brother Clayton will wet his pants. The CFO of Powell & Cooper."

"Already thinking about introducing me to your family, huh? And here I was thinking you still had a bunch of catching up to do."

"Fuck that, Katherine. We've wasted enough time." Her voice is suddenly serious.

"Shall I call my dad and tell him to book the earliest flight to New York?" I slip from the bar stool she uses as a kitchen chair. I'm suddenly struck by the intimacy of this conversation, no matter the subject, and whether we're being serious or not. I remember all the lonely Monday mornings when I got ready for work in my own apartment with its white walls and everything in its right place. The contrast with today is so big, it floors me a little.

"Maybe we should tell Grace and Anna first." Ali folds her arms around my waist. "Or no, let's do something else first, now that we've replenished our energy reserves." She lets her teeth sink into the flesh between my shoulder and my neck. "Turns out I'm still hungry."

"They'll be so smug about this, those two. According to Grace they called this that very first night we all met."

"Let them be smug." Ali traces her hands up to my breasts. "They were right, after all."

ALI

"You're in love with her now?" Anna sounds skeptical.

"Fuck yeah, Anna." I want to make sure she gets the message loud and clear that I'm in no way in two minds about this.

"When was the last time you really fell in love?" Why is Anna grilling me like this? I thought she would be pleased to hear about my passionate night with Katherine.

"I don't know." Maybe it's sad, but I truly don't remember. I shrug.

"Exactly," Anna says. "But now, all of a sudden, because Katherine professed her feelings for you, and you had this amazing night together, you're in love."

I chuckle. I suddenly get what she's doing. She's channeling Grace—Katherine's concerned best friend. I knock on the table. "Can I please have *my* best friend back?" I stare her squarely in the eyes.

"I'm sorry, Ali… I, er, we are worried that Katherine's still fragile. We just want you to be sure."

"Now that you've started talking as the Royal We, you can tell Grace that my intentions with Katherine are nothing but pure."

"That might be so, and it might all be very exciting right now, but what's going to happen a few months down the line, when that initial spark starts subsiding and you're left with… what you had before?"

I shake my head. "I can't predict the future, Anna. Nor can Katherine. But we have no choice but to take that leap of faith."

"Oh, I know." Anna relaxes her shoulders. "I didn't mean to put you on the spot like that. But we're all such good friends now and, well"—she holds up her hands—"I know how completely selfish this is going to sound, but we want you getting along at our wedding."

"Looks like you're going to have to take the leap of faith with us then." I can so easily predict what kind of an emotional wreck organizing this wedding will make Anna. If anything, she should enlist Katherine, who is very good at bossing people around and getting things done.

"I do take the leap, Ali. I really do. I'm so happy for you."

"As you should be. Grace told Katherine that you two"—I make air quotes with my fingers—"'called it' that first night she and I were re-introduced."

Anna thinks about this for a minute. "Yeah, that's right. There was this thing between you, probably caused by the fact that you had a history, and Grace and I were so completely besotted with each other that it was the only logical conclusion we could draw at that point. Though you sure took your time."

"It's different with her. Because we've become such unlikely friends first. I learned to appreciate all her good sides *and* her quirks long before we got together." I look into my wine glass for inspiration to finish my little speech. "It's like we did all the hard work already and now all we have to do is sit back, relax, and enjoy the fact that we took this next step."

Anna nods thoughtfully. "Was it not odd to suddenly find yourself in bed with one of your best friends?" She cocks her head. "Did it translate to that setting?"

I think about this for a second, but all I can do is break out into a wide smile and shake my head. "No, it was perfect. What was odd, however, was how easily I started seeing her as a lover instead of a friend. Like a switch had been flipped. Katherine can really turn the flirting on when she wants you, I'll tell you that. When we were on that date, she was nervous at first, which I had expected her to be, because she has that kind of personality and she had made the first step and so on. But when she started breaking out of her shell, and realized we were actually on a date—and she was on a mission—she went for it. She fired and she sure as hell didn't miss."

"I can't stop telling you how good this news is on so many levels. Now Grace can stop looking for viable candidates for Katherine to date. And *I* can stop worrying about you."

"Why would you worry about me?" This snags my attention more than anything else she has said.

"Because I always believed you had the next level of happiness within your grasp," Anna says solemnly.

"What are you talking about? I was perfectly happy before this. You know I'm not one of those people who need to be in a relationship to be happy. I've always been perfectly content on my own."

"I'm not saying you weren't happy, Ali, but tell me honestly, aren't you over the moon right now?" She lifts her eyebrows and looks at me triumphantly.

"Oh Christ. The Couples Lobby has done quite a job on you since you got with Grace." Of course, I have to admit—even if it's just to myself—that now that Katherine and I have taken the next step, I do, in fact, feel over the moon. Though I'm well aware a large part of that is the hormones swarming my bloodstream.

"You don't have to tell me just to humor me, Ali. I can tell just by looking at you." She gives me a big grin.

"Yeah, yeah." I find her gaze. "Just so we're very clear on something. Katherine and I will not be wearing matching dresses at your wedding. Come to think of it, I don't think I'll be wearing a dress at all."

Anna draws her lips into a pout. "We'll see about that."

CHAPTER TWENTY-FIVE

KATHERINE

I'm at the office. It's almost five and I'm actually contemplating going home early when the intercom buzzes. "Yes, Jane?"

"There's a Miss West to see you. She doesn't have an appointment and she's not a client."

"What?" Fear and something else mingle in my stomach. "Ali West?" I ask, ridiculously.

"Yes, Alison West."

"Okay, send her in. Why don't you go home early tonight, Jane?" I make it sound like an instruction more than a question.

"Sure," my assistant says.

Then I'm left with a few seconds of silence before Ali is shown into my office. Of course, she's been in the building before. I brought her here and she dated Mia, who has moved on and joined another company years ago.

The door opens and despite Ali's arrival being announced, I jump a little.

"Miss Shepherd," she says, her hand outstretched but a wide smile on her face. She closes the door behind her.

"Ali." I can't reprimand her for coming here, though it's highly inappropriate. "What are you doing here?"

She looks around and whistles through her teeth. "I wanted to see where you spend most of your waking hours."

Then she turns around and parks her behind on the side of my desk. "And I wanted to see my lady, of course."

"Did, er, you see Jane leave?"

Ali frowns. "Jane? Your assistant out there?" She points at the door with her thumb. "What does it matter if she left or not?"

"I'm not in the habit of bringing women up here." As I say this, I know I'm not handling this well, but Ali has caught me completely off guard.

"I would certainly hope not." Ali flashes me another smile. She knows me well and is not fazed by my reaction. "But I'm here now, so let's make the most of it."

Before I can even reply, she has jumped off the desk and is leaning over me, peppering kisses on my neck and cheek.

"Ali, come on," I grumble, but don't push her away. "This is my work place. Anyone could walk in."

"How about I lock the door?" she whispers in my ear. "And then I fuck you while you look out over Manhattan."

I don't even have a suitable response to that. But what I do have is a tingle in my belly and a rush of happiness through my veins just because she came to see me. My discomfort is quickly fading away to make room for something else. Extreme horniness by the looks of it.

Ali locks the door and strides back to me with that confident gait she has. The fact that she's walking towards me causes another uprising of butterflies in my stomach. I'm so completely besotted with her, I'm seriously entertaining the notion of having sex with her in my office. I'm not only entertaining it, I'm giving in to it. I want it. Because it's her.

"Stand up," Ali says, and it's more an instruction than a question as well.

Stricken by lust, I do as I'm told. Ali holds my gaze and it's enough to make me drench my panties. My clit is already pulsing against the constraints of my underwear. She'd better make this quick.

"Stand by the window with your back to me." Ali's voice is breathy. This is turning her on greatly as well. It's been three weeks since our date and all we've done in our spare time is have sex. Ali likes to use the term *fucking each other* but I still have problems using the f-word outside of the bedroom.

Again, I do as I'm told. My window looks out over a bunch of buildings and Central Park in the distance. It's still very much light outside and though I'm pretty sure nobody can actually look inside, standing here makes me feel uncomfortable.

I can't see her, but I feel her behind me, even though she's not touching me. "Hike up your skirt," Ali says.

I could be snarky and ask why she doesn't do it for me, but I'm guessing she has a certain mood in mind for this and I don't want to ruin it. So I tug my skirt as far over my thighs as it will go.

"Higher." Her breath is in my ear. She's so close but she's not touching me.

I struggle with hoisting it all the way up to my hips, but succeed in the end. If I'd known she was coming over, I would have worn something more amenable.

"Panties down, legs spread." Ali's tone of voice is in no way threatening, and I know I could turn around at any time and look into her smiling face—no matter what she had in mind for this—but this is turning me on immensely, so I quickly push my panties down and spread my legs.

"You may want to hold on to the window for support," she says, then sinks her teeth into the exposed flesh of my neck.

I let my hands fall against the window. There's not much reflection, but enough to make out Ali's movements. Not that I need to see to know what she's doing. A finger trails up my inner thighs, soon zoning in on my pulsing, wet lips.

Jesus Christ. Falling in love with Ali already felt so

totally out of my comfort zone, but this is like stepping into an entirely different world. This is my office. I will never be able to look out of this window again without thinking of this, of her. Maybe that's what she set out to achieve.

Then I stop thinking, because Ali has inserted two fingers and, with her other arm, reaches over my thigh to find my clitoris.

She gives me a few slow strokes first, but then ramps up the pace of all her fingers. We can hardly engage in a drawn out lovemaking session while I have my hands up against my office window. Nor can I enjoy the view, because I'm enjoying what she's doing to me too much. I already know she's going to hold this over me later. "All I had to do was walk into your office, give you a few looks, and you were so ready," she will say, and I can already hear the words now in my head, and they turn me on even more.

"Come for me, Kat," she says, and if I weren't already putty in her hands, I would be now. I don't mind that she calls me Kat, or Katie, or Pussycat. Ali can call me whatever she wants. "Come for me," she repeats, and it sounds as though she's using her singing voice. There's an irresistible melody to the three words she keeps repeating, like it's a song she wrote especially for me.

And then I do. I come for her, while her fingers invade me from behind, and her thumb is on my clit, and she's all over me, so how could I possibly resist?

"Fuck," I scream out a little louder than suitable for the setting, when the climax sweeps through me, and leaves me with trembling limbs and weakened muscles.

When I turn around, my skirt still hiked all the way up, Ali puts her hands on my thighs and says, "Come home with me so we can finish what we started."

ALI

"I wrote you a song," I say, one Saturday night when Katherine is staying at my place. She always ends up staying at my place.

Her eyes widen. "You did?"

"Of course I did." I give her a mushy smile. "My heart floweth over with you and I always write about what's in my heart."

"Aw." She slants her head. "Will you play it for me?"

"If you're good." I sink my teeth into my bottom lip. In a flash, this could turn into us fucking again—fucking on the sofa, on the floor, in the shower—because I certainly can't get enough of Katherine. But I really want to play her this song. I've sung for her before, but never one of my own songs, not in a setting like this.

"When am I *not* good?" She crosses her bare legs.

"When you made me late for work yesterday morning," I say with a chuckle.

"You can't go to work," Katherine had said, "I haven't fucked you yet." I melted into her embrace instantly.

She draws her lips into an offended O. "That was just me reading your thoughts. How is that not being good?"

I nod and start playing the intro. "It's called "The Road To You" because it took you so damn long to realize how you truly felt about me, probably since that very first time you saw me in Seabolt's office." I give her a big grin, then play the song, which talks about taking the long road home and missed opportunities and taking chances and all that sentimental stuff I normally wouldn't want to be caught dead writing a song about. But with Katherine, everything is different. It just came to me one night when she was working late. I grabbed my guitar and the song just fell out of me, like all I had to do was be the vessel for it to come into existence. Now it exists, and I'm playing it for her. While my fingers pluck the strings, and I give her my most heartfelt rendition—because I can't sing it any other way—I keep my eyes on her. On Katherine Shepherd. The most unlikely woman for me. And now I've only gone and written her a song.

When I'm done, she claps and gives me one of those looks that could either mean she wants to drag me to the bedroom straight away or is about to say something deep.

"That was so beautiful. I feel so honored."

"If the subject is beautiful, it's not hard to make the song beautiful." Mere weeks ago, I would have gagged if I heard someone say something silly like that, but now the words freely flow from my own mouth—and I don't feel ridiculous at all.

"How do you do it, though? How do you create something that previously didn't exist?" That's the thing with Katherine, she always wants to know, wants things explained to her in the greatest possible detail.

All I can do is shrug. "I can't explain it, really."

"Indulge me." When she says it in her low and sultry voice, her chin resting on her palms like that, I have to at least try to put it into words.

"With a song like this, it feels as though all I have to do is show up for it. It will percolate in the back of my mind for a while and then all I have to do is grab my guitar and start playing and then it just comes. It's really strange."

"There has to be more to it than that." She looks mystified now. "Because what you're describing is genius at work."

This merits a loud chuckle. "I'm hardly a genius. I just… feel the music. I wouldn't call it magic either, but maybe just trust in my ability to write a song. Trust in the fact that if I make time for it and allow space for it in my brain to grow, then it will come out at some point."

"So you *are* a genius." Katherine gets up out of the sofa

and walks towards me. "You're *my* genius." She kisses me tenderly on the forehead.

"It has just always been that way, ever since I was a kid," I say pensively. "My parents tell me that even in kindergarten I used to spend my time making up songs, more than playing with the other kids."

"So you were a genius back then already," Katherine teases me.

"I don't think the teachers at 74th Street Kindergarten thought of me as a genius," I reply, "definitely more as an unruly child who wouldn't keep quiet."

Katherine is quiet for a moment. "You went to 74th Street Kindergarten?" she asks, a stunned look on her face.

"Yes... why?" I answer.

"I did too. For a couple of months at least. Before my father got transferred to another base." Katherine's face turns pensive and she muses, "Imagine if we'd met then. Would we have been friends, I wonder."

"I'm sure you wouldn't have been able to resist my charms, even then," I say with a flutter of my eyelids. "Well, you know, singing songs has always gotten me a lot of p—" I tease.

"Don't say it." Katherine sits down beside me. "Don't say the word, Ali. You're a changed woman now."

"Oh yeah? Says who?" I pull her to me and kiss her on the cheek.

"Who else have you written a song like that for?" She turns to face me. Her lips are so close I can almost taste them.

"No one." With a smile on my face, I very happily admit that I am, indeed, a changed woman.

CHAPTER TWENTY-SIX

KATHERINE

Instead of giving a speech, Ali has written a song for Anna and Grace's wedding. She's dressed in a pale blue suit which, truth be told, I had many reservations about, but I can sort of see it now that she's up on the stage, telling the band she doesn't need back-up. She hasn't sung a note yet, but I'm already beaming with pride.

This wedding has been a huge celebration of love all day long and I've found myself tearing up more than once. I'm guessing Ali singing for them now will be the crowning achievement. My tear ducts have no defense against her voice and the way she is when she sings—so free, so charming, so utterly gorgeous.

"I wrote this song especially for Anna and Grace on this day," she says after tapping the mic a few times. "My two dear friends who found love at Women's Week in Provincetown of all places."

A mild roar goes through the crowd.

"But they made it and here we are. Anna, Grace, I love you and I look forward to growing old beside you as your very lucky friend." She does the head tilt she always does before starting a song, then starts playing the guitar, and my eyes already fill just from hearing the intro chord, that's how much of an emotional wreck this wedding has made me.

I can't explain it. I've gone through a whole pack of

tissues throughout the day and I just can't stop. Of course, I'm really happy for Grace that she found the love of her life. But their union stands for something else in my brain as well. If they hadn't met, I wouldn't be with Ali right now.

We've been together for more than a year of intense bliss and it's as though I can only look back on it clearly today, at Grace and Anna's wedding. As though this day is offering me a unique looking glass to see my own life through.

What I see is a woman astounded by happiness. A woman come alive under the touch and love of another. After Susan dumped me so coldly, I was adamant to protect my heart, but Ali, with her unexpected tokens of friendship, her easy ways, and her slow smile, managed to not only make me fall in love again, but do so with a fierceness previously unknown to me.

I look at Grace and Anna holding hands, Anna's head resting on Grace's shoulder as they sway to the melody of Ali's song. Then I look at Ali, whose gaze finds mine, and she shoots me a little wink, and I feel it as though she actually just touched me instead of singing to a crowd of people.

Ali West, the girl I once despised, has not just conquered my heart, but my entire being, my life. It's been so easy since we got together. Not only because Ali is the most easy-going person I know, but also because with her, I'm my best self. All it takes to rid me of the stress of work when I get home is one of her lopsided smiles, and I'm ready to leave it behind. When she asked me to move in with her, I wasn't scared of getting my heart broken all over again, because it was Ali asking me and, when she looks at me, it feels as though she'll never look at another woman again.

Then there's the miracle of Ali's voice, which seems to reach unknown depths of me. When she sings, and she sings for me often, I always melt because it's such an essential part of her. Singing is in her blood and when she does it, pure happiness just radiates off her, like now. While she's singing for our friends and, I somehow just know this, also a little for me, she glows. When she hits a low note and closes her eyes in subconscious focus, she is so beautiful, so very much herself in the most exquisite way, it makes me fall in love with her all over again—and I was already so smitten.

Now, she's singing a high, long note, her chin tilted up, her entire body supporting her vocals, and when she looks back down and catches her breath, she looks at me again, and I think I might be asking her to marry me some time soon.

ALI

After I've finished my song for Anna and Grace, I hug them profusely, then head straight over to Katherine and whisper in her ear, "Come with me for a second."

Unlike me, she did put on the baby-blue bridesmaid's dress Anna and Grace asked us to wear. I don't know how she does it, but she manages to look stunning in it. By the hand, I drag her outside the ballroom, to the garden where, earlier, Grace and Anna exchanged vows and said "I do".

"You blew them away, babe," Katherine says and wraps her arms around my shoulders. "Not that I had expected otherwise."

"You were snivelling again," I tease. Katherine's been an uncharacteristically blubbering mess all day. When she gave her speech, she had to interrupt it twice to gather herself.

"I know. I don't know what's wrong with me today." She pins her blue gaze on me—that's how she can pull off this ridiculous dress. It brings out the color of her eyes.

"I do. You're overcome with love. Your best friend is

getting married to my best friend. It's overwhelming." I've been touched by it too, but I hide it better than Katherine. However, while I was singing, my gaze kept drifting to her.

"It's probably because of what they stand for in our history together. We sealed the deal because of them. We might not have met again if it weren't for them." Her eyes are going misty again.

"Don't be so sure of that. I think our paths would have always found a way to cross. Some things are just meant to be," I say.

"Is that what you dragged me out here to say?" Katherine plants a kiss on my nose.

"You know I've always had my very own way of saying things." My lips find her neck, then her earlobe. "I'm not sure I'll ever be the marrying kind, but I've never felt so close to anyone in my life," I whisper. Earlier, on stage, for the briefest of moments, the thought did flit through my mind, but I'm not one to go through all the pomp and circumstance Grace and Anna orchestrated today to officially make them a married couple. "I love you with every fibre of my being." Being witness to our best friends' love on display has made me go a little soft as well. "I hope you know that."

Katherine nods, her chin brushing against my cheek. "When you were on stage, even though I knew full well you were singing for Grace and Anna, it felt a little as though you were singing that song for me only."

I give a little chuckle, then start humming the chorus of "The Road to You" into her ear.

"Stop it, babe," she says, "you know what that song does to me."

I stop humming and start vocalizing, my lips so close to her ear. I know exactly what I'm doing to her. The song also reminds me of the weeks after we got together, after she told me how she felt about me, and the transformation it set in motion. Because now, when I sing, I do always sing for her, even when she's not in the room. I've seen her at her best and at her worst and, right now, while she's melting right before my very eyes as I sing her our song, Katherine is at her very best. She's relaxed, in love, and open to a lot of things she would have previously automatically dismissed, like my hand running from her bare neck, over the low neckline of her dress, all the way down, gathering the fabric at the knee, hoisting it up as high as it will go, and finding her panties.

"Oh Christ," she murmurs, but she doesn't stop me. She wants this. She wants me to do this to her at our best friends' wedding, even though it's highly un-ladylike, and very unlike the Katherine I first met. But here we are, both different people, somewhere in the middle of this road we're on together. I never looked for it and I certainly never thought I'd love like this but now, as I slip a finger underneath the panel of her panties, I know this is forever. I know because when I look at her, every single time, I feel it everywhere, not just in my heart, but all the way in the tips of my toes and fingers. And it was never my touch alone that made Katherine come alive like this, because she was like this from the very first time we slept together. All in. Ready to surrender. Consumed with more than mere lust.

As my finger enters her, the way it has done numerous times before, I feel a familiar heat travel through me. I'm still singing—I can drag this song out for as long as it takes—still have my voice in her ear and my finger inside of her and the moment is so perfect that, again, the thought hits me that, some day, I wouldn't mind being married to Katherine Shepherd, to this glorious woman about to fall apart at the touch of my finger again. A sight I can never get enough of. The way she tilts her head back, exposes her neck, contracts her muscles, and becomes mine in so many ways, I know I will write a million songs about it in the years to come.

"Oh Ali," she croons and, in my mind, it translates easily into "I love you."

I interrupt the song and say, "I love you too."

ACKNOWLEDGEMENTS

The idea for this book came to me after watching my wife's favorite movie (*When Harry Met Sally*) for the umpteenth time (and greatly enjoying it once again.) Admittedly, apart from the paths of my protagonists crossing over and over again, *The Road to You* bears absolutely no resemblance to the story it was inspired by, but what I'm trying to say in my usual long-winded fashion when it comes to things like this, is that this book would not exist without the ever-present support of my wife. After more than fifteen years together, she is still my main source of inspiration.

I owe a special shout out to beta-readers Carrie and Donna for making my Belgian English come across as more American and looking for New York-related inconsistencies. Thank you for your time and your help.

Thank you to my editor Lucy Felthouse, whom I worked with for the first time (in this capacity) and who did a great job of spotting my persistent weaknesses and offering editorial solutions.

Endless gratitude to the members of my Launch Team who keep coming through for me. I owe a special shout out to Sue and Susie T. for catching the last remaining typos and a heartfelt welcome to brand new and super-vigilant proofreader Claire J. (It really does take a village.)

Last but by no means least, a big hug to you, dear Reader. Your support and loyalty have changed my life.

Thank you.

ABOUT THE AUTHOR

Harper Bliss is the author of the novels *Far from the World We Know, Seasons of Love*, and *At the Water's Edge*, the *High Rise* series, the *French Kissing* serial and several other lesbian erotica and romance titles. She is the co-founder of Ladylit Publishing, an independent press focusing on lesbian fiction. Harper lives on an outlying island in Hong Kong with her wife and, regrettably, zero pets. She enjoys talking about herself and her writing process (but mostly herself) on her weekly YouTube broadcast Bliss & Tell.

Harper loves hearing from readers and if you'd like to drop her a note you can do so via harperbliss@gmail.com

Website: www.harperbliss.com
Facebook: facebook.com/HarperBliss
YouTube: youtube.com/c/HarperBliss